THE WILDERNESS COLLECTION

THE DISCOVERY COLLECTION

The Discovery
Ambush at Cisco Swamp
Armoured Defence
The Dinosaur Feather

THE WILDERNESS COLLECTION

Call of the Wild
Dino Champions
Dinosaur Cove
Eruption!

THE WILDERNESS COLLECTION

RANDOM HOUSE AUSTRALIA

A Random House book
Published by Random House Australia Pty Ltd
Level 3, 100 Pacific Highway, North Sydney NSW 2060
www.randomhouse.com.au

Robert Irwin, Dinosaur Hunter 5: Call of the Wild first published by
Random House Australia in 2013
Robert Irwin, Dinosaur Hunter 6: Dino champions first published by
Random House Australia in 2013
Robert Irwin, Dinosaur Hunter 7: Dinosaur Cove first published by
Random House Australia in 2013
Robert Irwin, Dinosaur Hunter 8: Eruption! first published by Random
House Australia in 2013
This omnibus edition first published by Random House Australia in 2014

Addresses for companies within the Random House Group can be found
at www.randomhouse.com.au/offices

National Library of Australia
Cataloguing-in-Publication Entry

Author: Irwin, Robert, 2003–
Title: Robert Irwin, Dinosaur Hunter 5–8: The Wilderness Collection/
Robert Irwin, Jack Wells.
ISBN: 978 0 85798 515 6 (pbk)
Series: Robert Irwin; 5–8.
Target Audience: For primary school age.
Subjects: Dinosaurs – Juvenile fiction.
Other Authors/Contributors: Kelly, Helen; Harding, David.
Dewey Number: A823.4

Illustrations by Lachlan Creagh
Cover and internal design by Christabella Designs
Typeset by Midland Typesetters, Australia
Printed in Australia by Griffin Press, an accredited ISO AS/NZS
14001:2004 Environmental Management System printer

Random House Australia uses papers that are natural, renewable and
recyclable products and made from wood grown in sustainable forests.
The logging and manufacturing processes are expected to conform to the
environmental regulations of the country of origin.

CALL OF THE WILD

WRITTEN BY JACK WELLS

RANDOM HOUSE AUSTRALIA

CHAPTER ONE

Robert's shoulders slumped. 'Are you sure?' he shouted through the heavy rain. 'Doesn't that pole go here?'

'I know what I'm doing,' Riley shouted back. 'That's where the longer one goes!'

Robert's older sister, Bindi, walked

over. 'Boys,' she said, shaking her head. 'Mum and I have our tent up, Riley's dad is unrolling his sleeping bag, and you two don't even have anything that resembles a tent yet.' Bindi pointed to the clump of canvas and the poles that lay on the ground between them. Rain puddles were beginning to form on top of it.

Embarrassed, Robert pulled the strings on the hood of his raincoat tighter around his face. The raindrops sounded like drumsticks tapping on his head. 'It's this rain,' he shouted. 'Everything is slippery and heavy.'

Riley nodded. 'It's getting dark, too. How are we supposed to see anything?'

'I don't know,' said Bindi, turning and running towards the ute. After pulling her rucksack out of its tray, she ran past and added, 'but you two had better learn to work together – and soon!'

Riley just stood in the gloom, rain bouncing off his shoulders. 'I think I've decided I don't like camping,' he muttered.

'C'mon,' urged Robert, 'let's show her we can do this.'

Riley sighed.

'Once we're in the tent it will be fine,' Robert assured him. 'We can tell ghost stories, read comics by torchlight, play card games . . .'

Riley still didn't move. He regretted the day his dad had agreed to go camping with the Irwins. The rugged Queensland outback had sounded like fun, but now . . . He looked up at the sky and sighed, before holding out his palm. 'Hang on,' he said, brightening, 'I think the rain's stopping!'

'Awesome,' cheered Robert. 'Let's get cracking!'

As the weather improved, so did their spirits. In no time at all, Robert was unzipping the front door of the tent, and he and Riley were unrolling their sleeping bags inside it.

Sharing a tent was as fun as Robert had predicted. After getting settled, Robert turned on his torch to help Riley search his bag for some stowaway lollies.

That was when Robert's mum, Terri, stuck her head inside the tent. 'Finally, you giant turtles have finished!' she said. 'But no snacks yet, Riley, your dad's just started serving up dinner.'

The boys groaned and crawled out of the tent. The rain seemed to have passed, but they both kept their raincoats on just in case. In front of the three tents, a campfire was now blazing. Riley's dad, Scott, was spooning tinned stew into five bowls as Bindi buttered bread.

'Our first night may not have started well,' said Scott, referring to the rain, 'but at least we'll be eating like kings!'

Robert and Riley sat on a damp, fallen log beside the fire and looked down at their gloopy dinners. They didn't agree.

As Riley was cautiously placing the

first spoonful of dinner into his mouth, an animal howled in the distance. He jumped, spraying food into the campfire's flames.

'Aah!' Robert dropped his bowl and spoon with a clatter. 'Riley, you freaked me out! What's wrong?'

'Th– that sound,' stammered Riley. 'It – it . . .'

'It was only a dingo,' laughed Robert.

'What do you mean *only* a dingo?' gulped Riley.

'Don't worry, we're safe here,' said Bindi. 'Dingoes are nocturnal animals.

They're just calling to each other in the dark.'

Robert smiled at his friend. Sometimes he forgot that other families didn't know as much about animals as his did. The Irwins lived at Australia Zoo on Queensland's Sunshine Coast, where Robert had grown up around all kinds of creatures!

'The dingoes shouldn't come near us,' Robert whispered to Riley, as everyone else ate. 'Besides, you've seen much scarier animals than dingoes, remember?' Robert patted his trouser pocket. Inside it was his fossilised *Australovenator* (oss-tra-low-ven-ah-tor) claw. Somehow it had taken Robert and Riley backwards through time, where they had seen all kinds of real-life dinosaurs.

Riley shivered. 'Why do you always have to remind me about the man-eating dinosaurs?'

Soon it was pitch-black and everyone had finished their meal. 'We might as well turn in,' said Scott. 'Tomorrow's another big day. We all need to make sure we have a good night's sleep.'

'Who knows,' Terri added with a mischievous glint in her eye, 'if we stay out here we might get eaten by the dingoes.'

Riley shrieked and ran back to his tent at full speed. Robert followed after his friend, smiling, as the others laughed behind him.

CHAPTER TWO

The campers were soon snug in their sleeping bags. It wasn't long before the boys could hear Riley's dad snoring in the tent next door. 'He sounds like a tractor warming up,' chuckled Riley.

After finishing Riley's bag of jelly snakes, the boys were talking by torchlight when the silence outside was broken by another dingo howl. Riley sat bolt upright.

'Calm down,' said Robert. 'They aren't going to eat us.'

'Are you sure?' asked Riley. 'Their howling sounds so spooky.'

'Maybe, but they aren't doing it to scare us. If dingoes hunt in packs they need to talk to each other. Their howls are to tell each other where they are.'

'Hunt?' squealed Riley. 'What do they hunt?'

'Not people,' said Robert. 'Kangaroos, possums, maybe rabbits.'

'Oh.'

'Besides, we aren't going outside until the morning. We're safe here. Just try not to think about them.'

Riley stared down at Robert. 'Umm . . .'

Robert shone his torch in Riley's direction. 'Really? You need to go to the toilet again?'

'I'm sorry!' said Riley. 'I drank a lot of water to help me swallow Dad's stew.'

'Crikey,' said Robert, struggling out of his sleeping bag. 'Come on then, quick.'

The boys slipped into their shoes and raincoats before Robert quietly unzipped their tent flap.

Riley poked his head into the fresh night air. 'It's really dark. What if we get lost?' he asked.

'Well,' suggested Robert, 'we could copy the dingoes and call out to each other. What do you reckon?'

Riley nodded.

'But I don't want to wake everyone by yelling out your name,' said Robert. 'Let's come up with an animal call to disguise our voices.'

'Well, you're Robert Irwin, Dinosaur Hunter,' suggested Riley. 'Why don't we roar like a dinosaur if we get lost? That might help to scare the dingoes away, too.'

Robert thought back to their adventures together. They had met many fearsome dinosaurs but none had really roared at them. 'I'm not sure dinosaurs *did* roar,' said Robert.

'Yes, they did,' said Riley. 'I've seen it on TV.'

'But have you seen it in real life?'

Riley sighed. 'No.'

'Dinosaurs were reptiles. Think of the reptiles we have at the zoo,' said Robert. 'Most don't make any noise, and none of them roars.'

'I have it!' whispered Riley. 'Birds evolved from dinosaurs, remember? Let's go *cheep-cheep*. Dinosaurs probably did!'

Robert chuckled. 'Mate, can you imagine a *Tyrannosaurus* (tie-ran-uh-saw-rus) saying *cheep-cheep*?'

Riley thought for a moment. 'Hmm . . . maybe not.'

16

'I do like your idea, though,' said Robert. 'Let's use a bird call. But not *cheep-cheep*. We might wake everyone up thinking there's a flock of chickens loose in the bush.'

'True.'

'If you get lost, just whistle like a bird, okay?' said Robert. 'Then I'll know where you are in the dark.'

'Fine, but let's hurry,' said Riley, 'or the inside of our tent might end up as wet as the outside!'

CHAPTER THREE

They crawled out of the tent and into the still night. Robert shone his torch in front of their feet as they squelched through the wet grass. The campers had dug a small pit toilet earlier in the evening, but it proved hard to find in the dark. After walking in circles for a while, Riley finally found it.

Robert stood at a distance with his torch off for privacy. Then he heard a dingo howl again.

'Did you hear that?' Riley whispered through the darkness.

Robert was starting to agree that the dingo calls sounded spooky. He had to remind himself that the dingoes were only talking to each other. 'Riley, just hurry up.'

Robert clicked his torch on again and lit the area around him for comfort. For a second he thought he saw a large bone lying on the sandy ground, but it was only a tree branch. Even so, Robert tingled at the thought of what it could have been.

This wasn't just dingo country. Robert knew that millions of years ago it had also been home to many dinosaurs, including the legendary *Muttaburrasaurus langdoni* (mutt-uh-ba-ruh-saw-rus lang-doe-nee), named after the town of Muttaburra in Queensland, where its fossils were first discovered.

Robert swept the light back and forth across the earth in front of him, imagining he was the schoolboy who discovered the second ever *muttaburrasaurus* skull. But Robert knew how incredibly rare it would be to find a dinosaur bone above the ground.

'Whatcha doing?' whispered Riley, who was now standing beside Robert. 'Looking for dinosaurs?'

Robert laughed. 'How did you guess?'

'That's all you ever do,' answered Riley. 'You almost never go dirt bike riding, or play video games with me. You've already found one awesome dinosaur fossil, but I guess one is never enough!'

Riley was right. As exciting as the discovery of the *australovenator* claw had been, Robert was always on the lookout for more. One day he was going to be a palaeontologist and discover a new, gigantic Australian dinosaur like the *muttaburrasaurus*.

Robert yawned. 'I guess we should head back. I don't want to be stuck out here in the dark if it starts raining again.'

'Or if a dingo shows up,' added Riley.

They started walking, but Robert couldn't find the canvas walls of the tents in the torchlight, anywhere.

'Are you sure it's this way?' asked Riley.

'I thought it was,' said Robert, doubtfully.

Another dingo cry split the night. Riley started walking much quicker. He was now in front of both Robert and the torch.

'Wait,' said Robert, jogging after him. 'If anything, I think their calls are getting further away.'

'Are you sure?' asked Riley. He stopped suddenly, causing Robert to run into his back. They both fell over, grabbing at the air for something to keep them upright. They landed in a ball on the wet ground, Riley on top of Robert, the fossilised claw in Robert's pocket digging firmly into his leg.

That was when everything went white and shimmery. Morning was a long way off, so what was happening? Robert and Riley started to feel extremely dizzy as the world began to spin around them. Robert shut his eyes to try to stop the sick feeling from growing.

Then everything stopped and all was quiet. Riley rolled off his best friend and landed on the wet earth with a *squelch*!

With Riley's weight off his chest, Robert sucked air into his lungs – air that was cooler and somehow slightly harder to breathe than he remembered.

'Did what I think just happen, happen?' asked Riley.

Robert sat up and raised his torch to get a better look at their surroundings. 'I think so.'

'Dinosaurs?' asked Riley.

Robert nodded. 'Dinosaurs.'

CHAPTER FOUR

Robert's glimpses of the plants in his torch beam told him that his *australovenator* claw had definitely transported them back in time. He pulled out his digital voice recorder and turned it on. As a scientist, Robert wanted to capture and keep all of his dinosaur-related thoughts and discoveries.

'I see lots of ancient plants,' he said. 'I think they're called *podocarps*, and a couple of ferns. They are very different to the gum trees we left in modern Queensland. Nearby, there is a small plant with a tiny flower on it. That means we have travelled no earlier than the early Cretaceous period.'

'How long ago is that, again?' asked Riley.

'About 146 to 100 million years ago.'

Riley smiled in the light of Robert's

torch. 'Wow, my dad wasn't even born then!'

They explored their new surroundings carefully, not wanting to travel too far but also too curious to stay still. They walked together, their rain jackets rubbing against each other's arms with a *zip-zip* sound. They were both glad to be wearing them. It had been raining here as well as back home, and the overcast night sky suggested it might rain again.

'You know,' whispered Riley as they walked, 'this is pretty spooky. There are no lights except for your torch. Even the moon is covered by clouds.'

Robert nodded. 'I know, but stop creeping me out. We have to stay positive.'

'I mean, I know dingoes don't exist here yet,' continued Riley, 'but what if there's a roaring, hungry dinosaur hiding behind those trees, just waiting for us to walk past?'

'I told you before,' said Robert, changing the subject, 'dinosaurs probably didn't roar.'

They walked on through mist that rolled around in the gloomy night air.

The dark outlines of a number of large animals flew over their heads and across the sky. Their shape told Robert they weren't birds.

'*Pterosaurs* (terr-o-sores)!' exclaimed Robert. 'Awesome!'

'*Terror*saurs?' gulped Riley.

'It's spelled with a silent "p",' said Robert. 'And the word means "flying reptile". They lived alongside dinosaurs for millions of years.'

'Speaking of dinosaurs,' Riley said with a shiver, 'what else might we see here?'

'I reckon we're still in Australia,' said Robert, 'so we might see a *Minmi para-vertebra* (min-mee par-ah-ver-te-bra) or a *Rapator ornitholestoides* (rap-a-tor or-nee-though-lez-toy-deez), but I'd really love to meet a *muttaburrasaurus.*'

Riley grabbed Robert's arm, directing his torch on a plant that had looked like a dinosaur in the dark. 'Were they meat-eaters?'

'No way!' answered Robert. 'But they were quite large and had a very recognisable face with strong jaws and a –'

Hoooonk!

Riley jumped. Robert froze. 'What was that?' they both whispered at the same time.

Honk! Hoooonk!

It sounded like an old car horn. But that was impossible! Traffic jams were at least 100 million years in the future.

HONK!

Robert pressed record again as they walked slowly towards the strange sound. 'We've heard something coming from a short distance away,' he said. 'It's a honking sound that I think could be an animal call, perhaps even belonging to a dinosaur.'

Robert stopped talking and held his recorder in the direction of the call in order to capture it.

HONK!

'Crikey,' he said, tugging on his reluctant friend's arm. 'C'mon! I have a feeling this is something we've just gotta see!'

CHAPTER FIVE

'Robert, wait,' called Riley, 'maybe we shouldn't. What if it's a giant meat-eating dinosaur? We could be its supper!'

'Whatever it is, it sounds scared to me,' said Robert.

Hoooonk!

'See?' Robert continued. 'I think it's

a small dinosaur, maybe even a juvenile. It's all alone.'

Riley looked sceptical. 'How can you know that for sure?'

'Well, it's a quiet call,' answered Robert. 'And listen, there isn't another honk coming in reply.'

They waited in silence for a moment, listening. There were no other calls.

'I think you're right,' said Riley. 'But let's go slow so we don't slip in a puddle or walk into a sleeping T-rex or something.'

Robert smiled. 'Okay, and I'll turn off the torch so we don't show ourselves.

But keep quiet. I don't want to frighten it. Just remember to make a bird call if we get separated.'

The boys trod carefully and quietly along the muddy earth. Every now and then they would walk past a clump of plants or pass under a tree. And then it was hard not to imagine a creature falling onto them or jumping out of hiding. Once or twice, Riley scared himself into thinking a tree was the leg of a gigantic sauropod (sore-o-pod).

The animal continued to sound its honking call, and still no reply came.

Robert wanted to honk back, just to let the poor creature know someone had heard it, but it wouldn't be safe to reveal themselves until they knew what animal was making the noise.

The call was getting louder as they continued walking closer. The ground was getting murkier, too. It was tricky staying quiet when each footstep made a *slurp* sound. Riley began complaining of water and mud seeping into his sneakers. Robert felt lucky he had chosen to slip on his hiking boots when they left the tent back in the 21st century.

It was very dark. Occasionally the drifting clouds would separate enough that a little moonlight seeped through and brightened their surroundings.

'Maybe you should turn on your torch,' said Riley, after he slipped on some mud.

Honk!

'Ssh,' said Robert. 'We're really close now. I think I saw it moving just beyond those trees.'

A few metres in front of them were two straight trees very close together. Beyond them, something was making sucking, squelching sounds.

Riley stopped and turned. 'On second thoughts,' he said, 'let's forget about this. I want to go find a *pterosaur* instead.'

'I think the poor thing's stuck in some mud, or a bog or something,' said Robert. 'We can't just leave it.'

They reached the two trees. While Robert held onto one for balance, Riley gripped the other for dear life. They both peered between the trees and at the shape of the creature that was struggling.

A bolt of lightning streaked across the sky, bathing everything in a flash of bright white light – long enough for the boys to see a small dinosaur, a little larger than them, with its legs stuck in a deep pool of mud.

Thunder boomed above them as the dinosaur stopped struggling to lean back and let loose another *honk* into the air.

'There's no chance it's being heard,' thought Robert. 'Especially with these thunderclaps drowning out its call.'

'What kind of dinosaur is it?' Riley whispered. 'And more importantly, is it a plant-eater or a meat-eater?'

Robert turned on his torch to get a better look, being careful not to shine the light into the dinosaur's eyes – it was terrified enough.

He saw four long limbs, but only the dinosaur's back legs were stuck fast in the mud. The dinosaur rested on its forearms, though it sometimes stood upright on its back legs alone. It had a long tail, a long neck and a small mouth. On top of its snout, above two large nostrils, was a bulge.

Robert gasped. Then he hid behind the tree and pulled out his voice recorder. 'What a ripper!' he whispered. 'We're standing 3 metres from a *mutta-burrasaurus*.' And partly for Riley's benefit, he added, 'It's a plant-eater, so Riley has nothing to worry about. I'd say it's only slightly taller than we are so I know it's a young one. Adults are a few metres taller and maybe 7 metres long. What a treasure from Australia's past! It's currently stuck in a deep mud pool. We'll have to somehow help it out.'

Riley's eyes snapped open. 'What did you say?'

The *muttaburrasaurus* turned and looked at the boys, following the sound of the strange voices it had heard.

Riley spoke quieter. 'How can we get it out?'

'I don't know.' Robert shrugged, 'but we have to try. It's tired and scared. How would you like it if you were left all alone?'

'Yeah, but . . . where are its parents, anyway?'

'I reckon its herd has been scared away, probably by predators.' Robert shone his torch over their surroundings.

'Look at all the footprints around us in the mud. Maybe they were chased along here but this little guy didn't have the strength to get through the mud pool. A predator would explain why the mother didn't stick around to help it out.'

Riley sighed. 'Okay, fine. But what's your plan for getting it out?'

It was a question Robert didn't have the answer to . . . yet.

CHAPTER SIX

With his torch guiding the way, Robert led them to the other side of the muddy bog. There, they were close enough to touch the *muttaburrasaurus*. Robert wasn't sure how long the young animal had been trapped, but it looked tired, and he guessed it was also hungry.

He shone his torch along the dinosaur's back and tail. Its beautiful, scaly skin was wet from the recent rain. 'It's okay,' Robert whispered, stroking the dinosaur's neck. 'We'll get you out of here, don't worry.'

The *muttaburrasaurus* flinched at first but relaxed as Robert spoke. Robert grinned. His *australovenator* claw had already given him some great adventures, but this was the first time he had had the chance to actually touch one of these amazing creatures. All his dinosaur books and TV programs would never seem as interesting again. He turned to Riley. 'Do you want to touch him?'

Riley recoiled like a spring. Robert had seen that same reaction many times before when an Australia Zoo keeper offered a visitor a touch of a snake or lizard. 'No, thanks,' said Riley, taking a step back.

Robert looked around. It was hard to get a sense of their surroundings in the darkness. He looked down, and could tell that the ground around the mud was firm but still very wet and sticky.

The *muttaburrasaurus* struggled again, before putting all its effort into a loud call that resonated from its snout and exited its strong jaws as a furious *HONK*!

Robert spoke into his recorder. 'This is hard to watch. We will have to try to push or pull the dinosaur out of the mud,' he said as it honked again.

'Push it out?' said Riley, covering his ears. 'Mate, I'm not strong enough to do that.'

'I think he just needs a nudge to help him on his way,' said Robert. 'He's strong enough to walk out, but needs to escape the suction around his legs.'

'Fine. But there isn't anything to grip. What if I fall in?'

Robert laughed at the thought. 'I'll pull you out. I don't think you'd be heavy enough to sink as fast as the *muttaburrasaurus* did, anyway.'

Riley threw up his arms. 'Okay then, Barry, let's try to get you out of here,' he said.

Robert smiled as he put his shoulder against the back hip of the giant reptile. 'Barry! I like that!'

Riley put his hands flat against the rump of the dinosaur, just over its tail. Surprisingly, Barry didn't try to shrug them off. Perhaps he didn't see any point wasting energy on these small, soft creatures.

'Okay,' commanded Robert, 'next time he lifts his front feet and tries to get out, push!'

The dinosaur tightened its muscles and rose up, trying to free itself from the mud's grip. The boys pushed with all their might, and just their small amount of added muscle power made a difference.

Though the *muttaburrasaurus* was still stuck, it had certainly moved forward a little!

Robert stood up and took a breath. 'Phew! One or two more pushes like that and I think Barry will be free.'

The boys resumed their spots, talking reassuringly to Barry while they waited for him to find the strength to try to escape again. When he did, they heaved against his side and back once more, helping Barry to get another step closer to the edge of the mud pool.

'Hooray!' said Riley. 'He's almost out.

Look, he can put his front feet on the ground!'

Robert was certain that having two of his feet on firm ground would have made Barry feel better, but they couldn't rest yet. Robert and Riley steadied themselves, ready to push one last time, when a long, pointed beak snapped at them from above.

Robert looked up to see two or three *pterosaurs* flapping their skinned wings in the night sky just above them. Riley shrieked and ran for cover among the trees that grew around the mud pool.

Robert was now alone in the dark with a frightened *muttaburrasaurus*. 'Riley! Riley!' he cried, but there was no response. The *pterosaurs* were still hanging around, threatening danger to both him and Barry. Robert took a deep breath before calling again. 'Riiileeey!'

Then Robert remembered their secret call. He pursed his lips and began whistling like a bird. Like Barry, he waited for an echoing response. But none came.

Robert sighed. 'Where in the world had Riley gone?'

CHAPTER SEVEN

The young *muttaburrasaurus* gave out a terrified honk as another *pterosaur* swooped down to get a closer look at him and Robert. They flew so quietly, Robert could imagine one taking Riley by surprise and flying off with him.

Robert whistled again, as loud as he

could, and shone the bright light of his torch in the direction he thought Riley had run. Robert turned to Barry, keeping one eye on the sky. 'I hope he hasn't slipped and fallen unconscious, or –'

'Robeeerrrt!' Riley shouted at the top of his lungs. He was running back towards Robert and Barry, screaming all the way.

'Riley!' said Robert. 'There you are! Where were you?'

But Riley didn't stop. He kept running past Robert and the mud pool, and off into the darkness. Robert looked up

to see a flying *pterosaur* zooming over-head, hot on Riley's trail.

Robert called out again. 'Be careful! You could get lost or slip over a cliff in this darkness!'

Riley turned and ran back once again. He was running to and fro, trying to lose his unwanted follower. Robert turned his torch on, both to brighten Riley's path, and to grab a glimpse of the *pterosaur*.

Riley ran past and hid behind one of the trees they had first watched Barry from.

Robert had his torch aimed upwards as the magnificent flying reptile came back. The light made the animal's scaly skin sparkle, and it almost shone right through its thin, metre-long, flapping wings.

Robert's torch beam trailed the *pterosaur* as it flew overhead. 'I can see the *pterosaur* has a long mouth, small eyes and a horn-like growth on the back of its small head.'

His torch accidentally shone in the *pterosaur's* face and startled it. It shook its head and closed its eyes to try to get away from the bright beam, before it turned around with a few vigorous flaps and flew out of sight.

Robert groaned. 'It's gone. I wanted to study it some more. But it was awesome while it lasted!'

'Are you crazy?' said Riley, emerging from his hiding place. 'I was going to thank you for saving my life, but if you even think about calling it back here, forget it!'

'Speaking of calls,' said Robert, 'why didn't you whistle? I was worried about you.'

Even in the dark, Robert could see his friend's head droop. 'I tried,' he said quietly, 'and then I remembered I don't know how to whistle.'

The boys laughed as the relief that they were both safe poured through them. Then Barry the *muttaburrasaurus* refocused their attention with another honk.

'Coming, Barry!' they shouted. The boys jumped over to Barry, who had been left to rest, half in and half out of the mud.

Robert stroked the dinosaur's neck.

'Crikey, mate, I'm so sorry. We'd forgotten all about you.' Barry turned his head towards Robert. He seemed to like the attention.

Riley took up his position behind Barry, as Robert leaned against the dinosaur's side. They both urged the young *muttaburrasaurus* to take one last step through the sticky mud.

Now that Barry's two front legs were on firm ground, he could help to pull while the boys pushed. After a couple of slips and a lot of grunting, Robert and Riley were soon standing next to a small, exhausted but free *muttaburrasaurus*.

The three of them stood still, studying each other in the darkness. Robert gave two big thumbs up to Riley. It was a bizarre feeling to know that they had actually saved the life of a dinosaur. But for Robert, helping others was always the right thing to do.

CHAPTER EIGHT

And then Barry ran away.

'What the?' said Riley. 'Barry, where are you – *come back*!'

Robert fumbled in his pockets for his torch. He'd had to put it away to help push Barry out of the mud pool. Now where was it?

The clouds in front of the moon parted, and for a moment the boys could see everything. Barry stopped about twenty metres away, rose up on his back legs, stretched out his neck and let out a long, haunting call.

The two boys approached the 'saur slowly as it ran back and forth, calling out the whole time.

'I think it's scared,' whispered Robert. 'It's lost and has no idea where to go in the dark.'

Clouds covered the moon once more. 'Turn your torch on,' suggested Riley. 'You might make him feel safer.'

Robert laid a hand on his torch and flicked it on, careful to shine it at the wet, leafy ground, and not in Barry's eyes. Barry was frantic, looking this way and that. He called out again.

Again there was no reply.

'It's so sad to watch how worried and scared he is,' said Robert.

'I would be too if I was in the middle of nowhere, all alone in the dark, with meat-eating dinosaurs on the prowl,' said Riley with a shiver.

'Hey, you're right!' said Robert. 'We can't hang around here forever. If he doesn't find his family soon, who knows what could happen to him. Or us!'

'What can we do?' shrugged Riley. 'We don't speak Muttaburra!'

'We have to try to help him.'

Riley scratched his head. 'How?'

Robert thought for a moment as they followed Barry, making sure to keep him in sight. 'Why don't we try to imitate Barry's call?' he said. 'We'd make it three times louder if we joined in.'

'Maybe we can separate a little,' added Riley, 'and get the sound travelling over a greater distance.'

'Great idea,' he said, 'but we only have one torch.'

'I'll be careful. Just keep doing the call so I know where you are,' Riley said.

Robert walked closer to Barry. In some ways, the *muttaburrasaurus* looked very similar to the crocs and other reptiles at the zoo. Robert smiled, thinking of home. Barry gave out a soft honk. 'It's okay, mate,' soothed Robert. 'We're going to help you find your mum.'

So with Robert a few metres to the left of Barry, and Riley a few metres to the right of him, they set off through trees and across the muddy, rocky landscape, in search of an adult *muttaburrasaurus*.

Robert tried his call first. He knew it sounded a bit more like a car than a dinosaur but he did his best.

Riley went next. 'That was very close to the real thing,' Robert thought to himself, 'but is it good enough to attract Barry's mum?'

Having the boys on either side of him seemed to give Barry some confidence. He walked onwards, staying between them and giving out a call every few moments. Robert continued shining his torch in front of them, and his calls improved with each one.

Again, lightning lit the sky. In the far distance, Robert thought he saw the long neck of a sauropod on a hill but he couldn't be sure.

'Don't wander too far, Riley,' shouted Robert. 'Who knows what's living around here in the dark.'

'You don't have to tell me twice,' said Riley. 'Let's just hurry up and get our little buddy home.'

CHAPTER NINE

They kept walking and were now nowhere near where they had first arrived in the Cretaceous period. Or were they? For all Robert knew, they could have been walking in circles.

'Robert,' called Riley, 'are you still there?'

Robert grinned. He remembered the bushwalks with Bindi when she was little. She would point out interesting birds or animals, but sometimes he'd lose sight of his older sister and would have to call out to her, too. 'Yes, Riley!' he answered. 'You okay?'

'I'm thinking this is crazy,' said Riley, after Barry had let out a rather long call. 'If his mum was nearby she would have called back by now.'

Deep down, Robert had to agree, but he couldn't give up yet. 'Honk!' he cried. 'Honk!'

The trio came to an area full of trees, covered in slippery leaves. Robert could hear Barry and Riley somewhere to the right of him. They each let out a long, loud call before it was Robert's turn again. 'Honk!' he cried.

Hooooonk!

Robert stopped. He slipped on some wet leaves and grabbed onto a nearby tree for balance. 'Riley!' he called. 'Was that you?'

'No, I thought it was you.'

Hooooonk!

It had to be another *muttaburra-saurus*! Its call was deeper and louder than Barry's but it was definitely similar. Barry ran towards Robert and let out one of his own calls. It was answered right away.

'Riley! Get over here!' said Robert.

But Riley was already on his way, heading for Robert's torch beam.

'Is it Barry's mum?'

Robert smiled. 'I think so.'

They slowly walked towards the sound and found themselves in a clearing. It was pitch-black and they still couldn't see the other dinosaur, but its calls were getting louder.

Then bolts of lightning flashed across the black sky, lighting up the earth. Against the sudden brightness, the figure of the adult *muttaburrasaurus* was clearly visible as it walked towards them. Then it rose up tall on its back legs, stretched out its neck, maybe seven metres high, and gave out an enormous honk as another lightning bolt split the sky behind it.

'Whoa! Awesome!' said Riley under his breath.

Barry trotted off towards his parent and ran under and around its legs before they turned to leave as a pair.

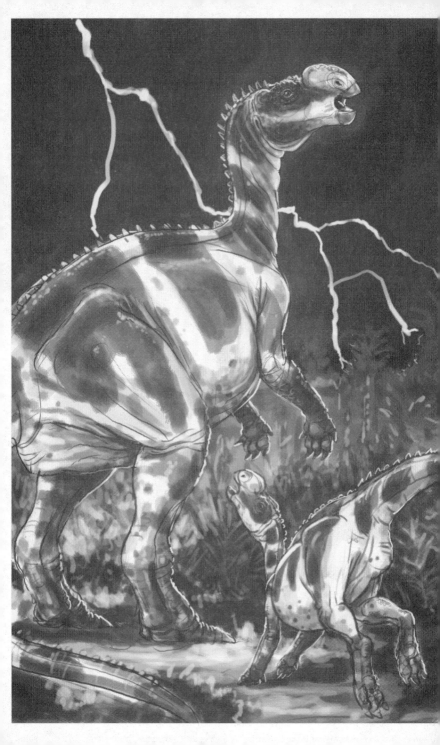

Robert started another voice recording. 'The young dinosaur has found its parent,' he said. 'The adult *muttaburrasaurus* who answered our calls is huge – maybe five or six times taller than Barry. The dome on the top of its long snout was helping it produce some of the loudest animal calls I've ever heard!'

The two boys stood and watched the two ancient Australians walk away to rejoin their pack. They were soon alone in the darkness, but they kept staring after the dinosaurs anyway. As a small honk drifted across the night sky, Robert

81

wanted to believe it was Barry saying goodbye and thank you. Then Robert's thoughts quickly went back to his own mother and family. 'It's late,' he said. 'Let's go home.'

Riley nodded and yawned in agreement.

CHAPTER TEN

'But how exactly are we going to do that?' asked Riley, as they walked back the way they had come under the light of Robert's torch.

'We need to find water,' answered Robert. 'That usually gets us back.'

'I never would have believed dinosaurs honked,' Riley mused.

'Well, that's just one dinosaur's call, there would have been others,' said Robert. 'Palaeontologists have uncovered many dinosaur skulls with features that may have helped them to make sounds. I still think lots of 'saurs were silent, though.'

'And to think I always thought they roared!' laughed Riley.

'Not many things do roar,' said Robert. 'Lions do, and –'

There was another bolt of lightning and then a tremendous rumble as a clap of thunder boomed overhead.

'Oh yeah, and thunder roars, too,' said Robert, putting his torch in his pocket and taking out the *australovenator* claw.

'Wait,' said Riley. 'Why did you do that? I can't see.'

Robert raised the hood of his raincoat and put an arm around Riley. 'I think that water we needed is about to arrive!'

Suddenly, it was as if every cloud turned on its tap. Rain poured down in sheets. Early Cretaceous Australia, along with Robert and Riley, was bathed in a torrent of water.

It was hard to see in the middle of the night-time storm, but Robert could sense that everything was beginning to go blurry and wobbly, as they were pulled forwards through time. The familiar, funny feelings waved through his body. A few moments later, everything felt normal again.

'Hey, what are those strange lights?' asked Riley, pointing ahead.

It was still dark and the rain kept pouring down, but a few lights were now bouncing around a short distance away.

'I think we're back,' said Robert.

They ran through puddles towards the lights. Terri, Bindi and Scott were carrying camping lanterns as they ran around the camp site, trying to secure all the odds and ends that were being blown about in the storm.

'Our tent!' cried Robert. He and Riley ran up to it. It had been flattened by the rain, and was soaked through.

'Your tent sprung a leak,' said Bindi, through the hood of her raincoat.

Robert and Riley's shoulders sank.

'Boys! There you are!' shouted Scott. 'Where in the world have you been?'

The boys stood silently in the rain as the three others gathered around them. How were they going to explain this?

'We called and called,' said Bindi, 'but you didn't answer!'

Robert looked at the ground. Maybe it was finally time to tell everyone their secret.

But before Robert could speak, Riley interrupted. 'Sorry,' he said. 'I needed to go to the toilet and we got a little lost.'

'You sure did,' said Terri. 'I didn't know we had to hand out maps to show the way to the pit toilet.'

Everyone laughed.

Later, dry and warm, Robert lay under a spare blanket. With one tent soaked through, he had been forced to share with his mother and sister while Riley slept with his dad. Robert lay in the dark, listening to the rain rattle on the thin roof. He thought of Barry and his mother, glad they were reunited, but sorry they didn't have a roof over their heads, too.

Robert yawned. He glanced at Terri and Bindi in their sleeping bags and smiled. 'At least Barry and his family are together,' he told himself. 'Being together is the most important thing.'

Robert closed his eyes, happy that he, Riley and Barry had each found their way safely home.

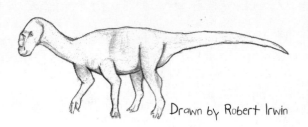

Drawn by Robert Irwin

MUTTABURRASAURUS

SCIENTIFIC NAME: *Muttaburrasaurus langdoni*

DISCOVERED: 1963 at Rosebery Downs

   Station near Muttaburra, Queensland

ETYMOLOGY: Named after the town

   Muttaburra and its discoverer,

   Doug Langdon

PERIOD: Early Cretaceous

LENGTH: Approximately 8 metres long

HEIGHT: Approximately 6 metres tall

WEIGHT: Approximately 2.8 tonnes

Scientists know *Muttaburrasaurus*

better than any other

Australian dinosaur, after *minmi*.

Despite being forever linked to the Muttaburra region, its fossils have been found in other locations, too.

Muttaburrasaurus was able to walk on two or four legs. The middle three fingers on its front legs were joined together to make a walking pad.

Its head was wide at the back and pointed at the snout, with a large rounded bulge on top. This would most likely have been used to create sounds, and also possibly for display.

Its jaws were very powerful and its teeth were designed to chew through tough plants like cycads.

Many Australian ancient history museums now have muttaburrasaurus displays. Why not go check out these amazing creatures for yourself?

WHAT SOUNDS DID DINOSAURS MAKE?

Despite what you see in the movies, scientists agree that most dinosaurs were silent, and it is likely none could roar. Dinosaurs would have mostly communicated through visual means (showing their colours, frills, horns, sails and feathers), or by making sounds like hissing, clapping, splashing, stomping or wing flapping.

It is true that birds, which make all kinds of sounds, evolved from dinosaurs, but the sirynt vocal organ that produces their calls evolved very late in history.

A small number of dinosaurs, however, are believed to have been able to produce definitive calls. Like *muttaburrasaurus,* these dinosaurs had features in their skulls that would have helped make the sounds audible.

Lambeosaurus, for example, had a hollow crest on its head that could have been used as a mini echo chamber to produce low calls. Duck-billed dinosaurs, on the other hand, had different facial features that could have made sounds, such as bellows, honks and rumbles.

Interested in finding out what Robert does when he's not hunting for dinosaurs?

Check out www.australiazoo.com.au

DINO CHAMPIONS

WRITTEN BY JACK WELLS

RANDOM HOUSE AUSTRALIA

CHAPTER ONE

Robert's legs were tired, and it was getting harder to breathe. He wanted to stop running. 'Come on, almost there,' he panted, urging himself on.

By the time he finally crossed the finish line, Robert was spent. He bent over, his hands on his knees, and gasped for air.

Robert's athletics coach, Eric, looked up from the stopwatch he was holding. 'You should stand up. I know it's hard, mate, but you'll recover more quickly.'

Robert groaned as he stood up tall.

Eric glanced down the track at the other kids who were still running, then turned back to Robert. 'You ran a good time,' he said encouragingly. 'Two minutes active rest then go for another lap.'

Robert nodded gingerly. He hated the words 'active rest', which was just another way of saying 'keep jogging'. It wasn't really a rest at all.

Robert started a slow jog along the inside of the running track. As hard as it was, he still loved athletics. It kept pushing him to be better, stronger and faster. 'Faster,' thought Robert. 'How am I going to get faster for next week's carnival?'

Sometimes it seemed like some of the other kids at athletics had been *born* faster – especially Lauren Johnson. She was a tall girl about a year older than Robert. She made running look so easy, and he had spent every training session over the past four months trying to catch up to her.

Watching Lauren run always reminded Robert of *Dromiceiomimus*

brevitertius (dro-mee-see-o-my-muss bre-vi-tur-tee-us), one of the fastest dinosaurs to ever exist. Its two legs were very long and built for speed, just like Lauren's.

Robert had done all he could to improve his running time. Eric had given him lots of 'aerobic exercise' to improve his breathing, and the strength training they did on Tuesdays had helped too. His leg muscles had definitely become stronger after doing that!

Robert smiled. He was proud of how far he had come over a short period time. He jogged up to the start line on the running track, and as soon as his foot landed on it, he broke into another sprint.

The wind swept his hair back as the red track blurred beneath him. He turned the first corner, the second, and then up ahead Robert saw Lauren.

'Come on, let's catch her,' Robert thought to himself.

His legs spurred him forward as he breathed the way Eric had taught him to. He was getting closer! Robert swung his arms back and forth even harder.

But it was no use. Lauren crossed the finish line. Robert finished soon after, panting for air.

'Wow, Robert!' shouted Eric. 'Your best time ever. Well done! Cool down and you can finish up, mate.'

Robert grinned. He might not be able to control how long his legs are, but he could control his effort!

After stretching, Robert walked to the stands overlooking the athletics field. As usual on a Thursday afternoon, his best friend, Riley, was sitting in the shade, waiting for training to finish.

'I think you're getting faster,' said Riley, and offered his water bottle to Robert.

'Thanks,' said Robert. He stopped to guzzle some water. 'Why don't you come down and join in next time?'

Riley shook his head. 'I've told you before. I get enough exercise running away from dinosaurs.' He patted the concrete beneath him. 'I'm happy to just sit here and watch.'

Robert laughed. It was true they had lots of experience running away from dinosaurs, thanks to Robert's mysterious *Australovenator* (oss-tra-low-ven-ah-tor) claw!

CHAPTER TWO

'Speaking of my claw,' said Robert, 'where's my bag?'

'Relax,' said Riley. 'I've been keeping an eye on it. It's here.' He threw the bag over to Robert. 'And be careful what you say – people will wonder what you're talking about!'

Riley was right. Robert hadn't told anyone else about the claw and how it could send them back in time. He searched through his sports bag, riffling through spare clothes and water bottles until he found the *australovenator* claw. It was there, safe and sound.

'Who's that girl?' asked Riley, pointing at the track. 'Doesn't she ever stop running?'

'That's Lauren,' said Robert. 'She's amazing. I'm catching up to her but she's still way faster than me.'

'She looks kind of like those tall, fast dinosaurs,' said Riley. 'I forget their name.'

'That's what I thought!' Robert said with a chuckle. 'Lauren's a regular *dromiceiomimus.*'

Riley scratched his head. 'Yeah, one of those.'

Other mini-athletes were now practising high jump, shot-put and discus on the grassy area encircled by the running track. The two boys sat and watched them for a while, grunting like gorillas whenever a good throw or jump was made.

'Crikey, I think we'll do well at the carnival next week,' said Robert, after one boy's particularly long discus throw.

'Why aren't you in any of the other field events?' Riley asked.

'Running is my best bet for a ribbon,' said Robert. 'I'm not as strong in the arms or shoulders as I am in the legs. I'm going to be in a lot of races, though.'

'It's like I said before,' said Riley. 'Running away from savage, meat-eating dinosaurs is good training!'

'Sometimes I pretend I'm being chased by a *Tyrannosaurus* (tie-ran-uh-saw-russ) or a *Spinosaurus* (spine-o-saw-russ) during training,' Robert admitted. 'It makes me run just that little bit faster.'

'Which one's a *spinosaurus* again?' asked Riley.

'We haven't seen one yet,' answered Robert. 'They're bigger than a T-rex and probably the biggest carnivorous dinosaur of all time!'

'Carnivorous means they ate meat, right?'

Robert nodded.

A shiver ran up Riley's spine. 'What was the biggest *plant*-eating dinosaur?' he asked, eager to change the subject.

'There are a few contenders,' said Robert. 'It might have been the *Argentinosaurus* (are-jen-teen-o-saw-russ).'

Riley chuckled. 'Imagine having a few of those guys on your athletics team! The other clubs would have no chance.'

'I reckon! Though it does take more than strength and size to be good at running or shot-put.'

'Well, I'd love to see some of the dinosaur champions,' said Riley. 'The fastest, strongest 'saurs would leave all the human champions in their wake. They would win every gold medal at the Olympics for sure!'

'Yeah,' said Robert. 'They couldn't help but be good runners and jumpers – it's just how they were built.'

'It would be pretty incredible to see!'

Robert raised an eyebrow. 'Mate, a minute ago you were scared to death of dinosaurs. Now you want to give them medals!'

Riley started digging around in Robert's bag. 'Where's that claw?' he said. 'I want it to take us to see the Dinosaur Olympics!'

Robert zipped his bag shut. 'Careful, it's fragile! Besides, we can't disappear in front of the entire athletics team.'

Riley groaned.

'We should make a move,' said Robert. 'Mum will expect me back soon.'

'Do you think the claw could take us to see those dinosaurs, though?' Riley asked as they stood up to leave. 'The fastest and biggest, I mean?'

'I guess so. But when and where it takes us is not up to us,' said Robert. He guzzled the last of his water and put the empty bottle in his bag. 'But,' he said, winking at Riley, 'they don't call me Robert Irwin, Dinosaur Hunter for nothing!'

CHAPTER THREE

The walk back to Robert's home at
Australia Zoo was a long one but it was
always a fun time for Robert and Riley.
They would chat about their dinosaur
adventures before having an awesome
dinner with Robert's mum, Terri, and
his sister, Bindi. For Robert and Riley,

Thursday afternoons were even better than Fridays!

Riley was growling and stomping like a *spinosaurus* by the time they both set foot in the park behind the Zoo.

'Grrr!'

'Stop!' Robert laughed.

'Me, *spinosaurus*, eat *dromiceio-mimus* for dinner! Yum!' said Riley, chasing Robert.

'Stop chasing me, I'm already exhausted,' said Robert.

But Riley didn't stop. He chased after Robert across the grass. Robert swung his bag over his shoulder, running away as best as he could.

'Grrr! You no match for mighty *spinosaurus*!'

As Robert ran, he could hear his *australovenator* claw jiggling around in his bag. Then, just as he reached the other side of the park, Riley caught him and Robert felt the world shake and spin. The green of the grass and trees was replaced by a glowing whiteness, and everything disappeared.

Robert felt like he was running on air. Dizzy, he stopped and bent over his knees to stop his head from spinning. When he opened his eyes, Robert noticed the ground was different. He stood up and looked around. The plants were different too.

'Run, Robert! Run!' shouted Riley, from somewhere behind him, much louder than before.

Robert pushed his legs forward as he looked back. Riley was running at full speed now – with a dinosaur close behind!

As Robert ran across the hard ground, over rocks and around thin trees, he swung his bag to the front of his body and struggled to unzip it. He threw a hand inside and began floundering around.

'I hope you've got a steak in there,' puffed Riley, now running alongside him, 'or we'll never lose this guy.'

Robert's hand finally grasped the small, metallic object he was searching for – his digital voice recorder. Robert swung his bag around again and turned to grab another glimpse of the dinosaur that was right behind them.

'We're being chased by a dinosaur,' he said, almost out of breath. 'It's about twice as tall as us. Its long legs and neck make up most of its height. Its eyes are huge.' Robert began to slow down. He was tired and was finding it hard to talk and run at the same time. 'It's covered . . . in feathers . . . with long arms that look like wings . . . a toothless beak . . . Wait a minute. Riley, stop running!'

Robert ground to a halt, panting. He put his hands on his head to open his chest and breathed deeply.

But Riley didn't stop. 'No way!' he called out.

'It isn't chasing us,' yelled Robert, as Riley and the dinosaur zipped past him. 'It has no teeth! It can't eat us!'

'W-what?' stuttered Riley. He stopped suddenly, and the dinosaur that had seemed to be chasing them sidestepped Riley and continued to zoom towards the horizon.

'Whoa! Did you see that?' asked Robert. 'Fast running and fast thinking!'

Riley was huffing and puffing, his eyes glued to the long tail of the tall, skinny dinosaur. 'All I'm interested in,' he wheezed, 'is that it's getting further and further away.'

Robert laughed, dropping his bag to the ground and spoke into his voice recorder once again. 'I think my claw has transported us to what is now Canada in the late Cretaceous period, perhaps 75 million years ago. That had to have been a *dromiceiomimus*! It was so tall and slender, with a body built for running.'

'Whatever it was,' said Riley, 'here comes another one!'

Robert looked back over the land they had just run across. Riley was right. Another *dromiceiomimus* was on its way. Robert's scientific mind clicked into overdrive as he picked up his bag. 'Quick, let's get behind one of those trees. I want to see what it does!'

CHAPTER FOUR

Riley threw up his hands. 'Come on, Robert,' he whinged, 'let's not hang around here. Think about why that other *dromiceiomimus* was running. Probably to get away from a T-rex or some other giant meat-eater!'

'I don't think so,' said Robert.

'I mean, it's the right time and place for *tyrannosaurus*, but . . .'

'But nothing. Let's get out of here!'

'But,' Robert repeated, 'if the first one was being hunted, why isn't the second one running too? It's just walking around. I think it's watching the ground, looking for something to eat.'

Riley looked at the second *dromiceiomimus*. It was moving slowly with its large eyes scanning the ground. Every now and then, it lowered its long neck and pecked at something in the dirt.

'It's coming. Hide!' said Robert.

The boys took a tree each and watched as the tall reptile came closer.

'We are observing a second dinosaur and I'm now positive that it is a *dromiceiomimus*,' Robert said, whispering into his recorder. 'It has muscular upper legs that help it run at high speed, three claws on each foot to grip into the ground like running spikes, and we have seen evidence of it using its large brain to evade obstacles. If I remember right, they can run at over 60 kilometres an hour!'

The *dromiceiomimus* was now standing on a small mound of flat rocks to the left of the boys. It was eating something off the ground. 'If it doesn't want to eat us,' whispered Riley, 'what does it eat?'

'They're omnivorous,' answered Robert. 'They eat a bit of everything. I think this guy must be eating small lizards off the rocks.'

Riley scrunched up his face. 'Er, yummy.'

The boys stood and watched the dinosaur for a few moments before Riley turned to Robert again. 'You know, with its long legs, arms that look like wings and beak, it looks just like an ostrich or an emu. Except it's taller and has a tail.'

'You took the words right out of my mouth,' said Robert. 'And that's exactly what its name means – "emu mimic".'

'As long as we don't run into the crocodile mimic I'll be happy,' said Riley.

'It's starting to run in this direction,' said Robert. 'Watch my bag.'

'What?' A look of alarm spread across Riley's face. 'Where are you going?'

'I want to race! Back in a minute!'

As the *dromiceiomimus* sprang past, Robert shot off after it. Running alongside the magnificent creature, Robert watched how the dinosaur's feathered legs drove its body forwards. He could see that the *dromiceiomimus's* power wasn't coming from below its knees but from above them, and that its upper legs and abdomen were the muscles it was using the most.

It reminded Robert of something Eric had once said about good runners using their core muscles in the centre of their bodies, not just their legs. Robert had made a note to remember that tip for the carnival.

The *dromiceiomimus* turned its small head and blinked at him. Then, as if to challenge Robert, it sped up and pulled ahead of him, covering Robert in a puff of dust.

Robert stopped and watched the *dromiceiomimus* run ahead of him, just like Lauren did at every training session.

'Never mind,' he told himself, 'you won't have to race one of those guys at the carnival.' He smiled at the sight of the *dromiceiomimus* disappearing over

a hill, in awe of its speed and strength. Then Robert dawdled back towards Riley and the trees.

'You know,' said Riley, 'not many people have raced a *dromiceiomimus* before – and kept up with it!'

Robert laughed. 'You're right!' He unzipped his bag and took out his *australoventor* claw. 'I'm so lucky to have found this fossil!'

The two of them sat under a tree and took a few sips from Robert's extra bottle of water. Then they leaned back in the shade to rest.

And before long they were fast asleep.

CHAPTER FIVE

In the split second before Robert opened his eyes he knew something was wrong. The world was filled with high-pitched, terrifying sounds.

Robert's grip tightened around the *australovenator* claw. Where were they? Everything was different. Instead of leaning against a tree, he was resting against a boulder. The plants were different, the sky was darker. And those sounds!

Robert turned and shook Riley, who was still dozing beside him. The ground trembled as Riley sat up straight. 'What was that? What's going on?' he shouted.

'I think the claw has taken us somewhere else,' said Robert. 'Listen to that!'

Snorting grunts filled the air. There were definitely dinosaurs nearby – large ones by the sound of it – that were making a lot of noise and shaking the earth as they stomped around.

Riley listened for a moment before he pointed over his shoulder, wincing. 'They're on the other side of this boulder, aren't they?'

Robert nodded. The sounds were definitely coming from that direction.

Riley closed his eyes again. 'I'm going to go back to sleep. Maybe your claw will take us somewhere nicer.'

'Don't you want to take a peek?' Robert asked. He was always eager to learn something new about his favourite animals.

Riley shook his head, his eyes squeezed shut.

With a shrug Robert slowly rose to his feet until he was able to see over the large rock. His heart began to race in his chest. What Robert saw was so stunning he pinched himself to make sure it wasn't a dream.

'What is it?' Riley whispered.

At first, Robert couldn't say anything.

'Robert?' Riley was starting to worry. He scrambled up to stand next to Robert and they both stared ahead with their mouths open.

They watched as two *spinosauruses* squealed at each other, fighting over a large animal that was lying dead between them.

'*Spinosaurus*,' said Robert. 'The largest meat-eating dinosaur ever discovered.'

Riley shivered. 'Even bigger than *tyrannosaurus*.'

Robert swallowed. 'They're more massive than I was expecting!'

Apart from their size, two other things stood out to Robert and Riley

as they watched the dinosaurs battle. The first was the sail of spines that stood up on each of the dinosaur's backs. These spines were as tall as an adult and the two 'saurs waved them around as they stamped about on their two massive legs. The other special feature of *spinosaurus* was its long crocodile-like skull.

Robert pulled his eyes away and squatted down to get his voice recorder from his bag. He quickly returned to his position next to Riley and pressed record. 'We are now in northern Africa, about

40 million years before *dromiceiomimus*. We are watching two *spinosauruses* battle over their lunch. It's amazing! Unlike other large, carnivorous 'saurs, *spinosaurus* has straight teeth. Like crocodiles, they probably used these and their long snouts to catch fish and other sea creatures. This could mean we're near the sea.'

The *spinosauruses* were snapping their long jaws, their rows of straight teeth cutting at each other like sharp knives. Finally, one *spinosaurus* gave up the fight and lurched away as the victor began crunching the animal between its jaws.

'I just can't believe how similar their heads are to the crocs we've got back home,' said Robert. 'Australia Zoo's Graham has nothing on these guys, though!'

'And I can't get over those spines,' said Riley. 'What are they for?'

'They're for presentation, but probably to keep its huge body cool, too.'

'Well, it certainly *looks* cool,' said Riley. 'Not that I want to be friends with it or anything!'

'Uh-oh,' said Robert, turning his head. 'Don't look now, but I think we're about to make friends with the other *spinosaurus*!'

CHAPTER SIX

Riley slowly turned to face their new friend.

The *spinosaurus* that had lost the right to eat lunch had returned. While Robert and Riley had been watching the victor eat its lunch, the loser had come around from behind and was now looking at them from about the distance of the length of a running track.

'We're trapped!' yelped Riley.

The *spinosaurus* wasn't heading towards them yet. It seemed to be studying them. Robert decided to take a chance. He stood and studied the dinosaur back. Perhaps it wasn't sure if eating the boys was worth the effort. Maybe it had poor eyesight and wasn't sure what it was looking at. But it was most likely afraid of the other *spinosaur* on the other side of the boulder.

Whatever the reason, Riley wasn't going to hang around a moment longer. He pushed off his side of the rock and sprinted towards the cover of some trees a short distance away.

Robert reached out to catch his friend but was too late. 'Riley, wait!' he shouted.

The sudden movement hadn't gone unnoticed. The *spinosaurus* snapped to attention before bounding off after its tiny prey.

The dinosaur was huge, measuring around 18 metres in length and at least

5 metres high at the top of its spines. Its body was thin and crocodile-like, and it snapped its jaws in anticipation of catching Riley. But all that didn't put Robert off. There was no way he was going to just sit back and watch!

Though his entire body was tired, he managed to dig deep and find some extra strength to push on towards the trees where Riley would be waiting. Robert threw his bag over his shoulder and dashed off, cutting across the path of the *spinosaurus*. Now the terrifying 'saur had two targets to choose from.

Robert entered the trees. He hoped it would be harder for the *spinosaurus* to follow them among the tightly growing tree trunks, but he also knew that it would depend a lot on how hungry their hunter was.

He spied Riley leaning against a tree trunk and breathing heavily. Robert ran up to him. 'Come on, mate,' he said. 'We can't stop yet!'

'I can't do it,' moaned Riley. 'You're so much fitter than I am.'

'I might go to athletics,' said Robert, 'but no one is a match for a *spinosaurus*. Let's go!'

Robert pulled Riley off the tree and the two of them jogged deeper into the woodland. He made sure to keep talking to Riley, encouraging him not to stop. By the time they made it to an open clearing on the other side of the trees, all was quiet again.

'I think we've lost him,' said Robert, glancing back to make sure. 'Well done. You might end up on the athletics team, after all!'

'Ha-ha, very funny,' said Riley, collapsing onto the ground. 'I would never catch up to you, let alone to Lauren. You're stronger and quicker. Your batteries never run out – just like a dinosaur's.'

Robert lay down. 'Believe me, my batteries need a recharge,' he wheezed. 'That *spinosaurus* was so big and fast.'

'And scary,' added Riley.

Robert laughed. 'But you know, like me, you could learn how to be faster and practise to get fitter.'

'I guess so,' said Riley.

'And I don't think Lauren has ever run as fast as we did just now.'

Riley nodded. 'True. She's never competed at the Dinosaur Olympics!'

The boys lay on the ground, side by side, gazing up at the clouds as they caught their breath. The sky looked just like it did at home, until a small *Pterosaur* (tear-o-saw) flew overhead.

Riley sighed. 'I know that the more you do something, the better you get,' he said. 'But I don't care if I never have to practise being chased by a giant meat-eater ever again!'

CHAPTER SEVEN

Robert took out his voice recorder in order to catch up on all he had seen and experienced while being chased by the *spinosaurus*.

'I just realised,' said Riley, after Robert had finished, 'there isn't any grass here.'

'No, that appeared much later in history,' said Robert. 'It's weird, isn't it? We just take grass for granted.'

'I think my dad would be happy living here,' said Riley. 'He hates mowing our lawn.'

Robert finished the last of their water. He hoped they wouldn't have to do any more running before they got home. One of the first things he learned at athletics was the importance of hydration. He drank a lot more water now that he was a runner.

Robert put the empty bottle back in his bag. 'There must be a body of water somewhere near here,' he said, 'or these massive dinosaurs would die of thirst. I think we should go look for it.'

Riley's eyes opened wide. 'Are you kidding? I don't want to see another *spinosaurus*, thanks!'

'But whenever we've travelled back to prehistoric times, it's been water that has taken us back home. Remember?'

'Oh, yeah,' said Riley.

Robert zipped up his sports bag and stood up. 'We need to find some higher ground to scope out our surroundings. Mum will be starting to wonder where we are.'

Riley chuckled, getting to his feet. 'Don't worry, I'm sure she won't mind us stopping off in prehistoric Africa on the way home.'

As they headed towards a hill only a short distance away, Robert hoped they might be able to see some water from the top of it.

'We've already met two dinosaur champions,' he thought aloud as they walked. 'I wonder if we'll see any more before we leave.'

'Two is enough for me,' said Riley. 'Unless, of course, the winner of the

Smallest Dinosaur Award decides to show up.'

'Actually, I'd really like to see the biggest plant-eater,' said Robert.

'But we've already seen a *spinosaurus*,' said Riley. 'Wasn't that big enough for you?'

'The giant plant-eaters like *argentinosaurus* put even the *spinosaurus* to shame,' said Robert. 'They were even taller. A *spinosaurus* might be the 'saur you want for shot-put, but an *argentinosaurus* would just need to step over a high jump bar to break the record!'

Robert and Riley made it to the top of the hill. Looking around, it was obvious there was no water nearby.

'Maybe there's water on the other side of the trees.' Robert sighed. 'That could be the reason why we weren't chased all the way over here.'

'I'm not risking going back there just to look for water,' said Riley. 'Get out your *austrelovenator* claw. We need to go somewhere else.'

'But how?' asked Robert, as he pulled it out of his bag.

The claw was fossilised, hard like stone, but still easy to imagine on the hand of one of Australia's most deadliest dinosaurs. Riley took the claw and started rubbing it.

'It isn't a genie bottle,' said Robert, slightly amused.

He reached for the claw in Riley's hand. As soon as he touched it, everything began to spin. Robert and Riley held on tight to the claw.

'What's happeni-i-i-ing?' shouted Riley as they were sucked away to yet another time and place.

CHAPTER EIGHT

As soon as their new surroundings had settled, Robert looked around. They were in a lush, forested landscape. The air was moist, and in the distance mountains curved against the sky.

Riley started tugging on Robert's arm. His mouth opened and closed but no words came out.

'What?' asked Robert.

Riley, still speechless, pointed upwards. What Robert had originally thought was a mountain was actually *moving*. It was the largest living thing he had ever seen.

'That has to be a sauropod,' whispered Robert, awestruck.

It seemed to take them a minute just to look up and down the length of the dinosaur's body. The immensity of it was astonishing. After waking from their trance, Robert followed Riley to a hiding spot behind a tree.

'This is never going to protect us,' said Robert. 'That dinosaur is so big it could squish us and not even notice.'

'Then get your claw to take us away again,' demanded Riley. 'I don't want to get squished!'

Robert was about to try when the enormous dinosaur raised its long neck high into the air to chomp on an equally gigantic plant. 'Hang on,' said Robert, 'I think I've been granted my wish.'

'Is that the dinosaur from Argentina you were talking about?'

Robert nodded, taking out his voice recorder. He pressed record and spoke into it as the sauropod continued to feed, even closer to them now. 'Riley and I are watching a sauropod – I think it's an *argentinosaurus* – grazing on treetops. So we must now be about 97 million years in the past. The size of it is really unbelievable. I'd guess it's well over 30 metres long, with more than half its length made up of its long neck and tail. Its rounded body and four legs plod in between as it scans the world around it for food.'

Robert ventured out into the open to get a closer look at the giant.

'What are you doing?' Riley hissed. 'Okay, *so this* 'saur might be vegetarian, but what if some meat-eating dinosaur comes and attacks it?'

Robert pointed up at the *argentinosaurus*. 'What animal would attack *that*?' He laughed. 'I reckon the only danger facing this guy is the threat of running out of food. Imagine how much he needs to eat to keep going!'

Robert knew the *argentinosaurus* wasn't going to be a danger to them as long as they stayed out of its way. Riley groaned and cautiously followed his friend.

'When the *argentinosaurus* reaches up to eat the tops of trees, his head must be over 20 metres above the ground,' said Robert, continuing his voice recording. 'Even when bending down low, its mouth is over twice our height in the air.'

The titanic sauropod turned around slowly. Its body looked like a bridge with its two sets of legs as the supports.

'Wow,' Riley breathed. He nudged Robert in the side. 'I dare you to sprint under its belly. You could run with your arms in the air and do backflips and you still wouldn't be able to tickle its tummy!'

Robert chuckled but there was no way he was going to risk his safety by running around the legs of a dinosaur too big to notice him. One kick would see him fly as high as a pole vaulter!

Robert watched the *argentinosaurus's* mouth slowly make its way through a load of leaves and plants.

'We can learn a lot from Argie,' Robert said.

'What do you mean?' asked Riley. 'He doesn't look like he knows his times tables.'

'I mean, getting fit for the athletics carnival isn't just about putting in lots of hard work at training, it's also about what you put in your stomach. You need the right fuel.'

Riley groaned. 'Great! I suppose that means no more wedges with sour cream after school!'

CHAPTER NINE

Robert and Riley walked alongside the *argentinosaurus* as it searched for more food. They soon came across a river that flowed between the trees and other plants the *argentinosaurus* was devouring.

'At least it'll have plenty of water when it gets thirsty,' said Riley. 'That's also important when you exercise, right?'

'Yep.' Robert nodded. 'Apparently, you're already dehydrated when you begin to feel thirsty. Eric says it's important to drink water throughout the day, even if you aren't training for a carnival.'

As they continued along the bank, the river had grown wider and fiercer. The ground was becoming rockier too, and the boys soon arrived at a pile of rocks.

Robert took a step or two up the rocks before Riley stopped him. 'Where are you going?' he asked.

'I want to get a bit higher off the ground,' Robert answered. 'There's a large flat rock at the top that should give us a better view of the *argentinosaurus*.'

Riley grudgingly followed him, using gaps and overhangs in the rocks to climb on top of the rock slab, bringing them 2 or 3 metres higher than ground level. In front of them, the *argentinosaurus* ate peacefully. Behind them, the river roared past.

Robert and Riley watched in awe as the dinosaur turned, cracking a tree in half with its 10-metre-long tail.

'Hey, what dinosaurs were the swimming champions?' Riley asked. He was lying flat on his stomach, peering at the thundering water below.

'The aquatic reptiles that lived at this time were amazing creatures, but they weren't dinosaurs,' said Robert. 'I'm not sure if many 'saurs could actually swim.'

'I'm pretty good at swimming,' said Riley. 'Maybe I could join the swim team or something.'

'Well, why not start practising now?' said Robert, grabbing his friend's shoulders and pretending to push him over the edge.

'*Whoa* – hey!' squealed Riley. 'Don't you dare!'

Robert laughed as Riley sat up, gripping the rocks beneath him like a koala joey holding onto its mother.

Robert looked back at the *argentinosaurus*. It was now moving in the other direction, away from the river. He sighed, knowing he may never see a creature that big again.

'We should probably get going.' Robert eventually said. 'And that's the way home.' He pointed at the fast flowing river below.

'I'm not jumping off here!' said Riley, suddenly alarmed. 'It's way too high!'

Robert giggled, shaking his head. 'Don't worry. We'll climb down and walk back to where the water is calm.'

They clambered down the rocks and, finding a spot where the river was almost level with the bank, took off their shoes. Robert knelt down and took the *australovenator* claw out of his sports bag. He gripped it tight, hoping it would send them both back home. Carrying his shoes in his other hand, Robert stepped into the water.

Riley eyed the river. 'It looks cold.'

'It is,' said Robert, shrugging, 'but it's the way home, too.'

Riley dipped a toe in. 'I don't know about this,' he said with a shiver.

Robert waded out further. 'Hurry up, slow coach!'

They kept walking until the river was up to their knees. The water lapped at their legs like cold, slippery eels. Robert remembered hearing Eric say that swimming was a good way to help your tired muscles recover. He took a deep breath and dunked his head.

It wasn't dark and gloomy like he'd expected it to be. In fact, underwater it was bright white – almost blinding. Robert felt Riley grab his leg from under the water then everything started to spin.

For a moment Robert was afraid he had been sucked into a whirlpool. He closed his eyes to stop from feeling sick, and when he opened them again he was standing at the back entrance to Australia Zoo, the warm evening sun already drying his running gear.

'Robert!'

Robert glanced down to see Riley looking like a drowned rat. He was outstretched on the grass and still holding onto Robert's ankle. 'Riley! What are you doing down there?'

Riley let go of Robert's ankle and held up the sports bag. 'You forgot something on the river bank!'

'Oh, thanks,' said Robert. 'You're a legend!'

CHAPTER TEN

It wasn't until Robert was on the home stretch that catching Lauren became a possibility. As soon as the starting gun fired she had sped off, leaving all the other runners in her wake. It had been like watching a *dromiceiomimus* racing a pack of *argentinosauruses*.

By the time Robert was halfway through the last lap he had pulled into second place. And he still hadn't even set eyes on Lauren! Though Robert couldn't smile – he was concentrating on his breathing – he was happy. Finishing a distant second would still be an accomplishment to be proud of.

Studying the dinosaurs with Riley had helped him a lot. All week he had eaten healthy foods to give him energy. He had stayed hydrated and had concentrated on using his core muscles to run. The early nights had helped, too.

As Robert turned the last corner the crowd started cheering. He looked up and saw his mum, sister and Riley all standing and clapping. But why?

Then Robert looked ahead. With 100 metres to go, Lauren was only about 25 metres in front of him! And she was slowing down.

Robert dug deep for some extra energy. His legs found a boost as he imagined a terrifying *spinosaurus* behind him. With the finish line only 10 metres away, Robert could almost touch her!

Lauren turned her head slightly. Seeing Robert so close, she also managed to muster up extra speed. She raised her long legs even higher, stretched herself forwards . . . and won by a metre.

Both Lauren and Robert collapsed on the grass, panting. As the other runners finished, the crowd was still clapping and whistling. Robert hadn't won, but it had been an amazing race.

After giving Lauren a high five, Eric made his way over to Robert. 'That was amazing!' he said, smiling. 'You're on the way to becoming a champion!'

Robert grinned. He was a champ even without coming first. He owed a lot to his training, but what he had learned from the dinosaur champions had definitely helped, too.

When he returned to the grandstand, his cheer squad was full of smiles and hugs and high fives.

'That was terrific!' said Bindi.

His mum, Terri, was smiling with pride. 'If only you could clean your room that fast,' she said with a chuckle.

Robert hugged her around the waist and looked at Riley. Robert's sports bag was hanging over his shoulder. Riley patted it reassuringly to show that the *australovenator* claw was safe inside.

Robert winked in reply. Whenever and wherever his next adventure back in time with Riley was going to be, he couldn't wait to see what they would discover!

Drawn by Robert Irwin

SPINOSAURUS

SCIENTIFIC NAME: *Spinosaurus aegyptiacus*

DISCOVERED: 1912 in western Egypt

ETYMOLOGY: Egyptian spine lizard

PERIOD: Late Cretaceous

LENGTH: Approximately 12-15 metres long

HEIGHT: Approximately 5 metres tall

WEIGHT: Approximately 6 tonnes

Spinosaurus is widely considered to

be the largest carnivorous dinosaur

ever discovered. The first fossils

unearthed were destroyed during a bombing raid over Berlin, Germany in World War II. Thankfully, palaeontologist Ernst Stromer had documented the finds in 1915 for the benefit of future scientists. More *spinosaurus* skeletons have been uncovered since then, including what could be a second *spinosaurus* species in Morocco.

Besides its enormous size, the most striking features of *spinosaurus* are its crocodile-like mouth and the tall sail that runs down its back. Some scientists believe the tall spines on its back were connected by fat, creating a hump, but the majority think that skin connected these tall bones. *Spinosaurus's* sail could have been purely for display purposes, but some experts believe it could have also been used to keep the large body of *spinosaurus* cool on hot days.

Because of its many crocodilian features, it is thought that *spinosaurus* lived near or perhaps partially in water. Its teeth were perfect for catching fish. *Spinosaurus* would have been a scavenger as well, preying on small and medium-sized animals. A *pterosaur* tooth has even been found inside a *spinosaurus* fossil!

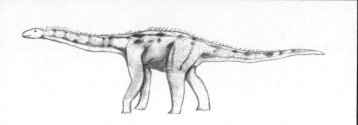

Drawn by Robert Irwin

ARGENTINOSAURUS

SCIENTIFIC NAME: *Argentinosaurus huinculensis*

DISCOVERED: 1989 in Argentina

ETYMOLOGY: Lizard from Argentina

PERIOD: Late Cretaceous, 97-94 million years ago

LENGTH: Approximately 36 metres long

HEIGHT: Approximately 7 metres tall from its foot to the top of its torso

WEIGHT: Approximately 100 tonnes

It is possible that *Argentinosaurus* was the largest dinosaur of all time. This would also make it the largest animal ever to live on land. The largest *argentinosaurus* backbones unearthed, from a sauropod in South America, were more than 1.5 metres wide and 1.7 metres long. These fossilised bones filled with minerals over time, and now each one weighs over 2 tonnes!

However, a complete *argentinosaurus* skeleton has yet to be uncovered. This means it is difficult to say for certain how big the dinosaur actually was. Based on the fossils that have been found and our knowledge of other *sauropods*, scientists can make an educated guess.

HOW DO WE KNOW HOW HEAVY DINOSAURS WERE?

Most dinosaur fossils that are found are bones. Soft tissues, such as skin, muscles and fat almost never fossilise. So how do scientists know how heavy dinosaurs like *spinosaurus* and *argentinosaurus* were when we only have their skeletons to work with?

The answer is: maths! Once scientists know the length of a dinosaur, they can determine its weight using lots of tricky formulae. One of the main difficulties in working this out is that the fossils of the giant dinosaurs (such as sauropods) rarely make up an entire neck or tail.

Those bones are just too long and fragile to survive! This makes deciding which dinosaurs were the biggest and heaviest a problem that scientists debate every day.

DINOSAUR COVE

WRITTEN BY JACK WELLS

RANDOM HOUSE AUSTRALIA

CHAPTER ONE

A scratchy voice came from the walkie-talkie. 'Three . . . two . . . one . . . Fire in the hole!'

BOOM!

Robert saw the explosion in the distance before he heard it. A thick spray of dust, rock and leaves was thrown into the air, and birds scattered across the sky. He knew visiting a place called Dinosaur Cove was going to be fun, but he had no idea it was going to be as awesome as this!

Robert looked over at his mum, Terri, and his sister, Bindi, both still covering their ears with their gloved hands.

Vicki, their guide, motioned that it was now safe for the group to put their hands down.

'Wow,' said Terri, 'that explosion was almost as loud as Robert singing in the shower.'

'Mum!' Robert groaned over Bindi's laughter.

After receiving clearance from the man on the other end of her walkie-talkie, Vicki turned to the group. 'Shall we go down and see the current dig site?'

Robert smiled and nodded vigorously.

'Careful,' said Bindi, 'it's freezing! If you nod any harder your beanie will fall off!'

It really was cold. It was the middle of winter, and being at the southern end of Victoria, Robert reckoned this was the coldest he had ever felt on his travels around Australia.

'It's more than freezing,' said Riley, Robert's best friend, as they began their short bushwalk, 'it must be a hundred degrees below zero!'

'I think the temperature's actually in the low teens,' corrected Vicki. 'If we walk quickly we should warm up.'

'It's hard to walk when you're so cold you can't feel your toes,' moaned Riley.

As they followed a trail through the bushland, Vicki explained that the area had yielded many important discoveries to palaeontologists. In fact, Dinosaur Cove was one of the very best places to look for dinosaur fossils in Australia.

'So why the explosions?' asked Riley. 'Won't that destroy all the buried treasure?'

'Actually, no,' said Vicki. 'We have to get deep into the rocks in order to reach the ancient layers that lie like stone blankets around the fossils. Here, I'll show you what I mean.'

They had arrived at a large opening in the ground. Coloured markers had been placed in and around the hole, with wooden steps leading down into the man-made cave. Once Robert was inside, he could see hundreds of divots in the rocks where stone had been cut away.

When everyone had gathered around, Vicki shone her torch along the walls to better show the different layers in the rock. 'The famous *Leaellynasaura* (lee-elly-na-saw-ra)', she explained, 'was found in an alcove similar to this one, not far from here.'

'Is that the dinosaur that has made many scientists question if dinosaurs were actually warm-blooded?' asked Robert.

'That's right,' said Vicki, impressed.

A cold shiver ran up Riley's spine. 'Brrr . . . I wish I was warm-blooded!'

'You are!' Robert laughed. 'So imagine how cold a reptile would be around here if it wasn't!'

'No, thanks,' said Riley, shaking his head. 'I only want to imagine a massive heater and me all toasty and warm.'

Robert didn't care about the cold. He put a hand into his back trouser pocket where he kept his fossilised

Australovenator (oss-tra-low-ven-ah-tor) claw. He touched it, wishing his next trip back in time would be to see the incredible *leaellynasaura* in action!

CHAPTER TWO

'You know, it's not as cold down here,' remarked Riley. 'But I am desperate for some hot chocolate.'

'Like I said, it's a good thing you aren't a *leaellynasaura*,' quipped Robert. 'They had to live in freezing temperatures all year round!'

'And they didn't have jackets or beanies to keep them warm,' said Bindi.

'Or hot chocolate,' added Terri, as Vicki led the group out of the cavern.

'I'd like to take you down a different track now,' said Vicki, pointing to a path through the bush. 'Down there is the site where *Timimus* (tee-mime-us) was first discovered.'

As they walked, the wind picked up and felt like ice against Robert's face. Even though he had gloves on, Robert stuffed his hands inside the pockets of his duck-down jacket.

'How did dinosaurs keep warm here if they were cold-blooded?' he asked Vicki. 'I've seen some with feathers. Did any Victorian dinosaurs have feathers?'

Before Vicki could answer, Riley interrupted them from behind. 'Uh, he doesn't mean he's seen feathered dinosaurs in real life, just in books!'

Robert turned and gave Riley a grateful smile.

Vicki laughed. 'I know that's what he meant, silly. Though, seeing one in real life would be a dream come true!'

'I'm sure it would be,' said Riley, knowingly.

Riley was the only other person who knew about Robert's mysterious *australovenator* claw. Robert had found it on a dig site in Winton, Queensland and, somehow, the claw had the power to transport them back to prehistoric times.

'Going back to your question about dinosaurs in the cold,' said Vicki, '*leaelly-nasaura* is certainly one small dinosaur that has given us all a giant headache.'

'Did you hit your head on the fossil?' asked Riley.

Vicki chuckled and shook her head. 'As Robert mentioned before, the assumption used to be that dinosaurs, like our modern-day reptiles, were cold-blooded. This means their bodies didn't produce heat like ours do and that they would have had to keep warm by staying in the sun or by being active.'

'Like our crocs back at the zoo,' offered Bindi.

'Exactly! Gigantic dinosaurs may have survived in cooler climates because their sheer bulk would have kept their body temperature high,' explained Vicki.

'But that little girl – *leaellynasaura* – was tiny. It's a puzzle as to how she could have survived living all year round within the freezing Antarctic Circle if she wasn't warm-blooded.'

Vicki was about to usher them into another hole that had been blasted out of the bedrock when Riley stopped. 'Hang on a sec,' he said, looking troubled. 'This is Victoria, not Antarctica!'

'Yes, but millions of years ago Australia was connected to Antarctica,' explained Robert, 'until they eventually split apart and Australia moved north.'

'Right!' said Vicki, surprised by Robert's knowledge. '*Leaellynasaura* lived here. But back then, "here" was in Antarctica!'

Riley shivered. Suddenly he felt even colder.

'Okay,' Vicki said, pointing to the cave entrance, 'who wants to see where a *timimus* fossil was found?'

Everyone did, except for Riley. 'I'm freezing!' he said, shivering. 'Can I sit this one out?'

Vicki pointed away to her right. The roof of a demountable building could be seen poking up through the trees. 'Our research centre is that way. You're welcome to rest there, if you like.'

Robert sighed and rolled his eyes. 'Come on, Riley, let's get you warmed up.'

'Don't worry, we won't go far,' said Vicki. 'You can catch up to us later.'

As the boys walked off, the rest of the group turned towards the cave.

'You know,' said Terri, '*leaellyna-saura* may have been a warm-blooded reptile, but I think, with Riley, we've just discovered the first cold-blooded mammal!'

CHAPTER THREE

Riley slumped on a sofa, grateful to be out of the cold. Robert, on the other hand, couldn't keep still. He explored the centre, noting that it was really just a few offices and some rooms with big tables and tools for working on prehistoric finds.

'Just think – any minute a palaeontologist might bring a newly discovered fossil through that door!' Robert marvelled. He hoped to one day become a palaeontologist and make his own ground-breaking discoveries.

'What's so exciting about that?' said Riley. 'We've seen *real* dinosaurs. That beats looking at old bones.'

Robert's eyes widened. 'You've just given me an idea,' he said, pulling his digital voice recorder from one of his jacket pockets. Then, from his back trouser pocket he took out the fossilised *australovenator* claw.

'What are you doing?' asked Riley.

Robert pressed record. 'If the *australovenator* claw will take us,' he said, 'I'm hoping to go back to the Cretaceous and find out once and for all whether *leaellynasaura* was cold-blooded or not.'

'Whoa!' Riley jumped up and grabbed the claw out of Robert's hand. 'Are you crazy? I'm already cold. There – *in Antarctica* – we'll freeze to death!'

Robert stopped recording. 'We have our warm clothes,' he said reassuringly. 'It'll be quick, I promise.'

Riley waved the claw in the air. 'But this thing doesn't always do what we want it to, remember? Sometimes it takes us to where we *don't* want to go, and other times it doesn't even work!'

'I know, but –'

'Besides, you can't really think dinosaurs were warm-blooded . . . hey!'

A bright light shone out from the claw, blanketing everything around them. There was no way Robert was going to miss this! He took hold of the claw with his left hand, and grabbed Riley's arm with his right.

It felt like they were going down a giant plughole. Robert closed his eyes and smiled. He knew that the spinning, sinking feeling meant that when he opened his eyes he would be standing millions of years in the past.

The frigid air snapped hard against Riley, enveloping him with a cold so intense he almost fell over. 'W-w-what's happened?' he stuttered through chattering teeth. 'Who turned off the heater?'

'Mate,' Robert said, zipping up his jacket, 'I think we're in Antarctica!'

'I can't believe it!' said Riley. 'I knew that claw didn't like me.'

Robert buried the *australovenator* claw in his jacket pocket before doing the same with his hands. 'If it will make you feel any warmer,' he said, 'just tell yourself we're still in Dinosaur Cove.'

Riley shivered. 'We shouldn't have come. If you need any proof that Vicki was wrong, this weather is it.'

Robert wrapped his scarf around his mouth and nose. 'You don't believe that dinosaurs lived here?'

Riley shook his head. 'I mean, I know they found the fossils, but they must have got the dates wrong or something. This is way too cold for lizards, crocs or any reptiles. They all live in warm places, remember?'

'But Vicki said that the 'saurs here could have been warm-blooded,' said Robert.

'Well, I'm warm-blooded and I'm f-f-freezing!'

Robert said nothing. Riley did have a point.

Suddenly, a pitter-patter sound could be heard coming at them from behind. Robert and Riley spun around. From out of nowhere, a tiny dinosaur – not even half as high as the boys – dashed past them and into a thicket of trees.

'Was that a thunderbolt or a dinosaur?' cried Riley, hiding behind his friend.

'I'm not sure,' answered Robert. 'Whatever it was, I think it just proved that Vicki was right!'

CHAPTER FOUR

'You know, I'm not just cold,' Riley said, 'I'm starving!'

'Tell me about it,' said Robert. 'We had lunch ages ago, and our bodies must be using a lot of energy just to keep warm.' Robert broke into a grin. 'But aren't you excited? There really are dinosaurs living here!'

Riley shook his head. 'I don't know, mate. That thing was going so fast I didn't get a good look. Maybe it was a dog or something.'

Robert burst out laughing. 'A dog? This is 110 million years ago!'

'Maybe we could at least get a drink by melting some ice,' said Riley, after his stomach let out a hungry growl. 'That's one thing Antarctica should have a lot of.'

Robert studied their surroundings. 'Melting ice could work,' he said, 'except there isn't any here!'

'Huh?' Riley looked around. 'You're right! I thought this was meant to be Antarctica. Where are the ice and the penguins?'

Robert pulled out his digital voice recorder, shivering as a blast of cold air hit him. He quickly zipped up his jacket and pressed record. 'We have been taken back to ancient Victoria,' reported Robert. 'My guess is it's the early Cretaceous period. We've already seen one small two-legged dinosaur. I estimate that it's pretty close to zero degrees Celsius. We won't be able to stay around for long without shelter.'

'Zero degrees sounds like Antarctica,' said Riley, 'but it still doesn't look like it.'

Robert stopped recording. 'At this time,' he explained, 'Antarctica and Australia were sort of rotated. Zero degrees is cold but, due to the position of the land, it didn't get anywhere near as cold as it does in modern-day Antarctica. Temperatures close to minus 90 have been recorded there.'

'I think we better stop talking about this,' Riley said, shivering, 'or I'll turn into an icicle.'

Robert chuckled then turned to look

around them, trying to come up with a plan. They appeared to be on top of a rocky hill, with trees on all sides. 'We should keep moving to stay warm,' he said. 'Let's go down and see if we can find a *leaellynasaura*.'

'If moving around will keep us warm,' said Riley, 'let's get cracking!'

The boys moved off through the trees that surrounded them.

Riley grabbed a tree trunk to steady himself. 'It's so weird to think of a forest in Antarctica,' he said. 'The past was a pretty strange place.'

The ground was wet from rain, and in some places, icy snow was piled up against a rock or a tree.

'At least that shows it can snow here,' said Robert, 'even if it isn't snowing right now.'

'If you are asking me to build a snowman with you, think again!' Riley laughed.

It was darker down the hill, with trees and rocks surrounding the lower land like walls. Most of the sunlight came in from an opening in the trees directly in front of the boys. There, the ground sloped downwards again, and they could hear the sounds of a trickling stream in the distance.

'I guess we go in that direction,' said Riley.

Robert nodded. 'Where there's water, there will probably be dinosaurs.'

He took a step forwards, but caught his foot on a tree root hidden under the snow. Robert stumbled and fell through the soft snow before rolling down a sharp slope. When he finally came to a stop, lying in the dark at the bottom of an incline, he couldn't see a single thing.

CHAPTER FIVE

'Robert! Where are you?' came Riley's voice from above.

Robert stood up slowly, stunned but otherwise all right. His head bumped against a low roof. 'I think I'm in a small cave or burrow,' he called.

Robert walked towards the entrance, bent over in the cramped space. There was a small but steep incline upwards to the opening he had fallen through.

Riley's head popped up at the entrance. 'There you are,' he said. 'Cool! You found a secret passage!'

'It's actually quite a bit warmer down here,' said Robert. 'Do you want to come down and defrost?'

Riley wrinkled his nose. 'I don't know . . . it looks dark. As cold as I am, it's safer out here than in a creepy dark hole.'

Just as Robert was about to assure Riley that it couldn't be safer, there was a sound from deep inside the cave – a brushing of something against the rocky floor.

'Robert?' whispered Riley.

'Shh! Hang on.'

Robert ducked his head and crept towards the sound. If something was there, it couldn't be very big. Robert scanned the darkness. Then, about a metre away from him, he saw two large glinting eyes staring back at him.

Robert froze. 'What the . . .? Whoa!'

A small dinosaur leapt from its corner and bolted past him, scampering up and out of the little cave.

Riley screamed. 'Argh! Let me down, let me down!' he cried. He jumped through the hole and slid down, landing at Robert's feet. 'I was wrong. It definitely isn't safe out there,' he said, panting.

Robert looked down at his friend, covered in leaves and dirt, and laughed.

Riley, squatting under the low roof, brushed his pants and jacket clean. 'What was that? I thought you'd warn me if a ferocious dinosaur was about to leap out at me!'

'Ferocious? It might be dark down here,' said Robert, 'but I'm sure the 'saur didn't even reach your waist!' Robert pulled out his recorder and turned it on. 'I think the small cave we're in was being used by a *leaellynasaura* as shelter,' he noted. 'At least, I think it was a *leaellynasaura*. It was dark but the size of it was about right. We'll have to look at it in daylight to be sure.'

'Even if dinosaurs do live here,' said Riley, once Robert had stopped recording, 'I still don't agree that they were warm-blooded.'

'Why not?' asked Robert.

'If dinosaurs lived in holes like this, they would have stayed nice and cosy without needing to be warm-blooded!' Riley smiled, clearly impressed that he had solved the mystery.

'That's true,' said Robert. 'From studying bones, palaeontologists know that some dinosaurs that lived in Dinosaur Cove hibernated through the winter, probably in burrows. *Timimus* was one of those.'

'See, I knew it!'

'But that's not the whole story,'

Robert continued. 'As far as the experts can tell, *leaellynasaura* didn't hibernate. There are no signs of hibernation in the fossilised bones that have been found. There was something different about those dinosaurs.'

Robert started crawling around in the dark. The cave was only a couple of metres wide and long. He kept a hand out to stop him from hitting his head.

'What on earth are you doing?' puzzled Riley.

'I just had a thought,' said Robert. 'If we found evidence of the dinosaur's lunch or nest we could learn how much it ate or whether it slept in caves like this. That could support your theory that they were cold-blooded.'

The two boys searched the cave but didn't find anything interesting.

'I guess the 'saur was only in here for a short time,' said Riley.

Robert nodded. 'Maybe he saw us and came in here to hide or something.'

'That means it wasn't a *leaelly-nasaura* after all,' said Riley. 'It was a *Scared-he-saw-us*!'

CHAPTER SIX

After clambering out of the hole, Robert and Riley were greeted by a line of tracks. Two small clawed feet had run away from the hole and off through the snow. They led across the hard ground towards the gap in the encircling trees the boys had seen earlier.

'It hasn't warmed up much, that's for sure,' grumbled Riley.

'Well, there are three things we can do to warm up,' said Robert, adjusting his beanie. 'We can cover up . . .'

'Done that,' said Riley, patting his thick jacket.

'We can eat . . .'

'Did that, too, though hot chocolate would have made me warmer.'

'Or we can keep moving.'

Riley groaned. 'I hoped you were going to say we could turn on a heater.' He looked down at the small tracks.

'All right, let's find the little guy, then,' he said. 'And quickly, because I'm telling you – it's a cold-blooded reptile so it must be freezing!'

'Warm-blooded!' said Robert.

The boys laughed, pretending to argue as they followed the tracks over the snow and hardened earth. The ground soon started sloping downwards and the sound of the nearby stream grew louder.

'How can you tell if a dinosaur is warm-blooded, anyway?' asked Riley.

'I'm not sure if we can without a scientist,' replied Robert. 'But if we

45

find a *leaellynasaura* thriving in this environment that will be proof enough for me that they weren't cold-blooded.'

'I guess so,' said Riley. 'Though I reckon we'll find it hiding in another warm cave somewhere.'

Robert shrugged. 'Maybe.'

He was walking more quietly now, scanning the environment for any trace of the dinosaur. He didn't want to scare it away again. Riley, however, found silence very difficult.

'The footprints are pretty small. Is that right for *leaellynasaura*?' asked Riley.

'I think so,' Robert whispered.

'Why is it called *leaellynasaura*, anyway?'

'The scientists who discovered *leaellynasaura*, Tom Rich and Patricia Vickers-Rich, named it after their daughter, Leaellyn,' said Robert.

'How cool! I wish my dad discovered a dinosaur.'

'Why?' asked Robert.

'Because I'd get him to name it "*Rileysaurus rex*"!'

Robert laughed. 'There are lots of quirky dinosaur names. The Riches also discovered *timimus*, which they named after their son, Tim. Oh, and the *Qantassaurus* (kwan-ta-sore-us) roamed around Dinosaur Cove, too.'

'Named after the airline?' asked Riley.

'Yep!'

The boys were soon overlooking a more open area of the forest. Green plants were abundant, and a small stream flowed along the forest floor. On their right, the land rose sharply into a wall of rock. Little waterfalls tumbled down its face, feeding into the stream.

Riley tugged on Robert's jacket sleeve. 'Look down there!' Below them, a metre-long dinosaur was dashing around and nibbling at one plant after another. It ran this way and that, eating little meals as it tried to outrun the cold. It was such a comical sight, the boys had to hold back their laughter.

'Is that the 'saur that scared me before?' asked Riley.

Robert nodded. 'And I know what it is!' he said. He quickly unzipped his jacket and took out his voice recorder. 'Now that I can see the dinosaur in daylight I'm sure it's a *leaellynasaura*. Its size and shape are right. It has an extremely long tail for its body – the longest known on an ornithischian (or-nith-iss-kee-an) – and very large eyes. It is running around on its two legs and is using its short arms to hold onto thin branches as it eats from them. About half my height, it's either warm-blooded or has a woollen jumper under its skin, because it's freezing down here in the valley.'

'Why is he moving around so much?' asked Riley. 'He looks like a top spinning around in a box.'

'Moving is one way to keep warm,' said Robert. 'And speaking of moving, I think we should go down there and take a closer look.'

Riley peered down the slope to the icy stream below, and sighed. It looked steep. 'Somehow, I had a feeling you were going to say that.'

CHAPTER SEVEN

Robert and Riley crept down the rocky slope, using trees and plants to hide their bodies and dampen their foot-steps. The *leaellynasaura* didn't seem to notice them. It was more interested in eating.

The boys sat behind some tree trunks

53

and watched it feeding on plants only ten metres away.

'So, after seeing firsthand a *leaelly-nasaura* surviving in this cold weather, do you agree now that it isn't cold-blooded?' asked Robert.

'Maybe,' Riley said reluctantly. 'I mean, maybe it just comes outside to eat and then it snuggles up in a warm cave somewhere.'

'But keep in mind this isn't as cold as it gets here,' whispered Robert. 'It's summer.'

'What!' shouted Riley.

Robert put a finger to his lips. 'Shh, you'll scare it away!'

Thankfully, Riley's shouting hadn't bothered the *leaellynasaura*. It walked down to the very bottom of the slope and started sipping from the stream.

'Sorry,' said Riley, 'but did you just say this is *summer*?'

'It must be,' said Robert. 'Antarctic winters are dark for months at a time. The sun doesn't shine like this.'

'Unbelievable! That means *leaelly-nasaura* has to live through even colder, darker days than this?' said Riley.

Robert nodded. 'Even more reason to think that *leaellynasaura* is warm-blooded.'

They moved quietly to sit on a large rock that jutted out a few metres above the stream, near where the small creature was drinking. Robert whispered into his voice recorder, his eyes not leaving the amazing animal for a second. 'We can see the large eyes and scaly skin of the *leaellynasaura* very clearly now,' he said. 'Their eyes have probably evolved to help them see better during dark Antarctic winters.' Robert stood up suddenly. 'Bonza! Another three or four *leaellynasauras* have just shown up!'

The boys watched the group of small 'saurs devour any plants the first *leaellynasaura* had missed. Soon, they were pushing each other, fighting over the best leaves and shoots.

'It's like watching scaly chickens battle over the last bits of grain,' observed Riley.

Robert scoped out their surround-ings. 'I want to take a closer look. Let's get off this rock and hide within the trees down the slope.'

By the time the boys were hiding among the ferns by the stream, the dinosaurs were officially at war. It was a scuffle of tails and screeches as too many animals fought over not much food.

Every now and then, the boys would see a *leaellynasaura* mouth or tail appear through gaps in the branches.

Robert sat still and quiet, transfixed. 'They're so active,' he whispered after a minute. 'There's no way cold-blooded animals would have this kind of energy in this weather.'

But Riley didn't answer.

Robert turned to see him huddled in a ball with his hands over his head. 'What are you doing?' he asked Riley, puzzled. 'Trying to stay warm?'

'No,' came Riley's muffled reply. 'I just don't want to get trampled on.'

Robert patted his friend on the back. 'It's fine, they're little and there are only a few of them.'

Just as he said this, a dinosaur tore through the plant life hiding the boys. It swiftly sidestepped them before disappearing into another wall of bush.

The ground began to tremble. Robert and Riley looked at each other in alarm. It seemed like there were more 'saurs on their way!

CHAPTER EIGHT

'Aargh!' Riley covered his face with his hands.

Robert jumped aside, out of the way of the mini stampede. He quickly reached into his jacket and pulled out his voice recorder.

'More dinosaurs have arrived,'

reported Robert. 'I'm trying to get a peek through the leaves but, now that there are about 15 dinosaurs here, all I can see is a blur of legs and tails.'

'They're about double the length of the *leaellynasauras*,' said Riley, trying to help. 'But they are still small for a dinosaur. I wonder if they came here because they heard the *leaellynasauras* fighting.'

Robert raised his arm across his face as the tail of one of the newly arrived dinosaurs shot through the leaves. 'I think Riley is right. The plants around here must be like pizza to these 'saurs!'

Riley's stomach growled. 'Actually, these guys remind me of other dinosaurs we've seen before. Are they theropods?' he asked, as they crawled a few metres back from the scuffling dinosaurs.

Robert nodded. 'Yep. I wonder if they might be *timimuses*.'

'The hibernating dinosaurs?' asked Riley.

'That's right.' Robert turned on his voice recorder. 'The fossilised bones of these dinosaurs, if they are *timimuses*, show evidence of fast and then slow growth, which probably means they hibernated in caves or burrows through the long and dark winter months.'

Riley leant in to speak into the voice recorder. 'Which could mean they were cold-blooded.'

Robert laughed. 'Or not.'

Suddenly, the rumble of stampeding feet echoed from downstream. The boys froze. More dinosaurs!

'That's it,' said Riley, getting to his feet, 'I'm outta here!'

He ran a little further up the slope

to hide behind a large tree, with Robert close behind. A couple of dinosaurs came into view and they, too, began fighting over the plants.

'More dinosaurs?' asked Riley. 'How many more are there?'

'This is another species,' said Robert. 'Notice that these 'saurs look similar to the others – they have two long legs for running, they're less than two metres long and one metre high – but these ones have shorter faces and beaks.'

'Beaks?'

Robert's jaw dropped. 'They're *qantas-sauruses*!'

To see so many active 'saurs in this cold was clear evidence to Robert that if these animals were cold-blooded, their bodies worked very differently to the cold-blooded reptiles in the modern world.

One of the *leaellynasauras* was standing only a couple of metres away from the boys, behind some thick plants. Robert realised that if he crept forwards a little, he might be able to reach through the greenery and touch the tip of the *leaellynasaura*'s tail.

'Hey, where are you going?' hissed Riley.

Robert held a finger to his lips.

Riley rolled his eyes and crept down through the plants and leaf litter to where Robert was squatting. 'I'm freezing,' he said quietly. 'If I just agree with you and say all these dinosaurs are warm-blooded, can we go home?'

'Shh!' Robert stuck his hand into the bush, eager to be the first person to feel a *leaellynasaura*'s scaly skin. He felt along the cold, hard earth below the bushes. It rose into a mound, but Robert stretched further.

'Does the dinosaur feel warm?' asked Riley.

'Yes, very!' said Robert. 'Hang on, something's not right. It's soft and hairy.'

'What? Please tell me it's a blanket!'

Robert pulled his arm back. 'No, it can't be. It's breathing!'

All the talk had made the *leaellyna-saura* scurry away downstream. Robert and Riley looked at each other and then gently pulled the thin branches of the plant aside. In the dirt below the bush was a hole.

'A burrow!' Riley gulped. 'Do you think it's another dinosaur house?'

'Maybe, but it's way too small!' said Robert, scratching his head.

The small head of a hairy animal appeared at the opening of the hole. It was dark brown and it reminded Robert of an echidna without quills. The creature, only about the size of a baby wombat, turned and looked at Riley.

'It wasn't me,' squealed Riley, pointing a finger at Robert. 'It was him!'

CHAPTER NINE

The strange furry creature turned and scurried through the plants.

'What in the world was that?' said Riley, bewildered.

Robert leant into the opening of the small burrow. 'I'm not sure, but I think I see something white down there.'

Robert buried his right arm inside it.

'What if there's another creature down there, ready to bite your arm off?' asked Riley.

'I doubt it,' said Robert. 'It would have been scared off like the other one. Besides,' he said, pulling out a small white sphere, 'look at this!'

'An egg?' asked Riley. 'Wasn't that a mammal? Mammals don't lay eggs.'

'It was a monotreme,' answered Robert. 'In our time there are only two kinds left – the echidna and the platypus – but there used to be others.'

He carefully placed the egg as far into the burrow as he could, mindful that it needed to stay warm to survive.

'Are you telling me that mammals, monotremes and who knows what else all lived at Dinosaur Cove alongside the dinosaurs?'

'That seems to be the case,' said Robert.

'And I suppose monotremes are warm-blooded?' continued Riley.

'Yes, though they are actually very similar to reptiles in many ways. They lay eggs, for one thing!'

'Well, I guess if mammals, monotremes and birds are all warm-blooded, a dinosaur could be, too,' said Riley.

Robert raised an eyebrow. 'Did you just say what I think you said? Are you ready to agree with me?'

'Yeah,' said Riley. 'What do I know about animals? I was only disagreeing with you to try to annoy you.'

Robert laughed.

'Congratulations, Robert Irwin, Dinosaur Hunter,' boomed Riley. 'You are the winner of the "Were They Warm-Blooded?" competition!' Riley whistled and clapped his hands.

'Shh!' said Robert, but it was too late. Startled by Riley's clapping and whistling, the dinosaurs fled in all directions. As a *qantassaurus* charged by, its tail clipped Riley's left leg, sending him flying backwards into the stream. The shock of the icy-cold water made him screech.

Thinking quickly, Robert pulled out his *australovenator* claw. He knew that Riley was in danger of frostbite or hypothermia if he stayed this cold for much longer. Robert stepped down to the water. 'Quick! Grab my hand,' he called. 'It's time to go home!'

Robert held the claw tightly and jumped into the water near his friend. He grabbed Riley with his other hand, and they disappeared in a flash of white light.

CHAPTER TEN

Terri, Bindi and Vicki appeared around the bend in the walking track. The boys, now outside the Dinosaur Cove research centre, were wet from head to toe, and Riley was shivering.

'What on earth . . .?' said Terri.

'W-w-we went for a w-w-walk to warm up,' explained a stuttering Riley.

'But we tripped and fell into a river,' added Robert.

'Bindi, in the research centre you will find a cupboard near the front door,' directed Vicki. 'Grab some towels for the boys – they must be freezing!'

Bindi nodded and ran ahead.

'We might find a change of clothes there, too,' Vicki said to Terri.

Terri and Vicki helped the boys stagger towards the small building. They were in such a sorry state that Terri and

Vicki started to laugh. Robert and Riley would have found it funny, too, if their teeth weren't chattering.

'I think you should have waited until summer to go swimming again,' joked Terri.

'Ha-ha, Mum, very funny,' said Robert.

'You know, it's strange,' said Vicki, 'I didn't even know there was a river around here.'

Bindi arrived with the towels under her arms. Robert gratefully threw off his wet jacket and began drying his hair. Riley was too cold to move, so

Terri just draped the towel over his head.

Back inside the research centre, the boys were able to borrow some clothes from two palaeontologists. Once everyone was warm and dry again, the group stepped into Vicki's office and she put the kettle on to boil.

'I'm sorry about the wait,' said Vicki, pouring the water into mugs filled with chocolate powder. 'Even warm-blooded creatures can't get too cold.'

Riley slurped at his hot chocolate and then smiled, sporting a new chocolatey moustache. 'Yummm.'

'Talking about the need to stay warm,' Vicki continued, 'that's the amazing thing about *leaellynasaura*. They were fighters – able to survive in terrible weather conditions without hot chocolates or duck-down jackets! In fact, we're hoping that means we might find proof that some species battled through the late Cretaceous extinction event here.'

'You mean some dinosaurs might have survived when all the others suddenly died out? And here at Dinosaur Cove?' asked Robert.

'It's possible,' said Vicki.

Bindi pointed at her brother. 'I can see what he's thinking,' she said. 'He's dreaming about going to the late Cretaceous!'

'Well, it's a nice dream, even if it's impossible,' said Vicki.

Terri laughed. 'You never can tell with Robert and Riley,' she said. 'After all, they did just fall into a river you didn't even know existed!'

Everyone else chuckled and sipped their warm drinks, but Robert was lost deep in thought. Would he ever get to see what ended the age of the dinosaurs? And could any species have survived it? He pictured the special *australovenator* claw deep in his pocket, and wondered.

Drawn by Robert Irwin

LEAELLYNASAURA

SCIENTIFIC NAME: *Leaellynasaura amicagraphica*

DISCOVERED: 1987 at Dinosaur Cove, Victoria

ETYMOLOGY: Leaellyn's lizard

PERIOD: Early Cretaceous

LENGTH: Approximately 1 metre long

HEIGHT: Approximately 50 centimetres tall

WEIGHT: Approximately 60 kilograms

Leaellynasaura was named after

Leaellyn Rich, the daughter of its

discoverers Tom Rich and Patricia

Vickers-Rich. Because of this,

leaellynasaura has a female name. In Greek, 'saura' is the feminine form of 'saurus', which means 'lizard'.

Leaellynasaura is thought to have been an ornithopod, and is a dinosaur with one of the longest tails in proportion to the rest of its body. It also had a large brain and two big eyes, both of which would have been helpful adaptations when living in the dark winter months in Antarctica.

Leaellynasaura is a key figure as scientists attempt to determine the physical make-up of dinosaurs. For *leaellynasaura* to have survived in very cold temperatures, it could not have been cold-blooded as today's reptiles are.

Whether it and other dinosaurs were warm-blooded or something different altogether is still a matter of debate between scientists.

* As a complete skeleton of *leaellynasaura* has not yet been discovered, there are many different opinions on the exact dimensions of the dinosaur. The measurements listed here are just one of those hypotheses.

HOW DID DINOSAURS STAY WARM?

When dinosaurs were first discovered, scientists believed that they were slow, turtle-like creatures that must have been cold-blooded like modern reptiles. Since the 1960s, however, scientists have revised this opinion.

Those who believe dinosaurs were warm-blooded point to the fact that dinosaur fossils have been found in cold places, that birds (which evolved from dinosaurs) are warm-blooded, and that the speed at which dinosaur bones appear to have grown is similar to that of warm-blooded mammals.

On the other hand, scientists who believe dinosaurs were cold-blooded say that giant dinosaurs, like sauropods, were so large they would have overheated if they were warm-blooded. They also point out that the poles weren't as cold when dinosaurs were around, and that dinosaurs lack respiratory turbinates (structures found in the skulls of warm-blooded animals to help them breathe).

So which is it? It is possible that some dinosaurs were cold-blooded and others were warm-blooded. There could also be a third option that we have not yet discovered. Perhaps dinosaurs were neither cold- nor warm-blooded but something different altogether!

ERUPTION!

WRITTEN BY JACK WELLS

RANDOM HOUSE AUSTRALIA

CHAPTER ONE

'Stop swinging it, Robert!' shouted Riley.

Robert twisted round yet again to see what was behind them. As the chairlift squeaked and swung, Riley held on for dear life. Heights were definitely not his thing.

'But look at that!' said Robert, trying

to take in the whole view. 'See all the trails where the lava has run down?'

He turned back, sending the chair swinging crazily again. Riley tightened his grip and squeezed his eyes shut until the seat was steady again.

'Just look down,' said Robert. He leant over the bar, causing their seat to tilt forward.

Riley gingerly opened his eyes to glance at the paths of the ancient lava flows beneath them. His stomach did a flip. 'It is pretty cool,' Riley grudgingly admitted. Then he saw a sight he'd been looking forward to. 'Hey, look, we're almost at the top. Get ready to jump!'

With his feet safely on solid ground, Riley felt better able to take in the view. It was still early morning on New Zealand's North Island but the boys had already been up for hours. It was the last day of their trip and, as usual, Robert's mum, Terri, had kept the best till last.

They were spending the day at Mount Ruapehu, or as Robert and Riley preferred to call it, Mount Doom! Not only was it the actual volcano used in *The Lord of the Rings* movies but it was also one of the most active volcanoes in the whole world. They were going to go all the way up to the top to see the huge crater lake that formed there between eruptions.

It was a tricky hike and quite a long one. The chairlift had got them started and they were already standing at about 2020 metres above sea level. The guide had told them that it would take about three hours to get up to the crater lake, just in time for lunch, and then another two or three hours to get back down again.

As the guide talked to the whole group about safety, Robert and Riley, hidden away at the back, double-checked their bags to make sure they had enough food and water. Robert also checked the batteries in his voice recorder.

Riley looked across at him. 'Why are you checking that? You won't be needing that here.' He chuckled. 'Even I know that there were no dinosaurs in New Zealand! For once we'll have a normal adventure, just like normal people.'

Robert didn't respond but grinned silently to himself.

Riley stopped smiling. 'Right, Robert? I've never heard of a dinosaur coming from New Zealand . . .' Riley looked at Robert suspiciously. 'Did you bring the claw?'

Robert took his *Australovenator* (oss-tra-low-ven-ah-tor) claw from his pocket and wiggled it in Riley's face with a grin. 'It's always in my pocket, Riley, you know that.'

The *australovenator* claw was Robert's most prized possession and had hardly been out of his sight since the day he'd found it, months ago, on a dig site in Winton, Queensland. Every time he looked at it, Robert was amazed all over again that it had such hidden powers as to send them back to prehistoric times, but he could see that Riley was not impressed.

'It doesn't mean anything is going to happen,' said Robert. 'You're *probably* right anyway. Why would anything happen here where there were *probably* no dinosaurs.'

'Probably?' echoed Riley.

'Well, you saw the tuatara at Auckland Zoo the other day. Sometimes they're referred to as living dinosaurs, and they've been around since the Cretaceous period,' Robert said casually. 'It was hardly here all on its own – there must have been others.'

Riley looked nervous. To be honest, climbing to the top of an active volcano was quite enough excitement without having to worry that at any moment he might be zapped back to the age of dinosaurs.

Robert looked at the *australovenator* claw in his hands. 'Remember when we saw *Leaellynasaura* (lee-elly-na-saw-ra)?'

Riley nodded. How could he forget!

'That was over three months ago – the longest gap between trips yet. I've been wondering if all the magic in this thing has been used up or something. What if that was the last time?' said Robert.

'Oh, that would be terrible!' Riley said in mock horror. 'Imagine never having to fight off a rabid T-Rex ever again. Imagine always knowing where you were and what year it was. How boring!'

Robert smiled. 'Or maybe we just imagined the whole thing?' he said, as he returned the claw to his back trouser pocket.

'You'd have to be a complete dino-nut to have dreams of such weirdness. So maybe *you* dreamed them but not me! They were real, all right,' said Riley.

The boys turned to face the guide, who was coming to the end of his safety speech.

'So,' said the guide, 'the most important thing to remember today is to . . . ?'

'Stay together!' chorused the group.

CHAPTER TWO

'Did you get all that, you two?' asked Terri, as the rest of the group started drifting off in twos and threes to start the hike.

'Loud and clear!' said Robert.

'Well, what are we waiting for? Let's get going!' said Terri. Shooing Robert and Riley off in front, she and Bindi followed on behind.

The boys wanted to spend as much time as possible at the crater, which meant there was no time for dillydallying on the way.

With one guide way up ahead and another dawdling at the rear to make sure no one got left behind, the boys could safely go at their own pace without stopping every three seconds for Bindi to take a photo with her new camera.

The weather was cool but sunny, and it was only when they looked up at the very top of the mountain that they could see a thin line of snow. Apart from a few struggling clumps of green shrubbery, the mountain was desolate. The volcanic terrain was 20 different shades of grey and gravel, with lumps of rock and stone piled up in some places, while other areas were completely smooth.

The three peaks of Mount Ruapehu looked magical with the sun reflecting on the snow, and it wouldn't have surprised either boy if a hobbit or an orc wandered past.

'It's like we're walking on the moon! There's nothing for miles around,' said Riley.

'You know, people can only climb up here without proper equipment when it's summer,' said Robert knowledgeably. 'In winter there's really deep snow and blizzards! It can even be like that in summer sometimes.'

'That's crazy. Do you think it's the snow and ice that stop the volcano from erupting?' asked Riley.

'I suppose,' said Robert. 'Though, that could be a problem on a day like today. I reckon this volcano could blow at any moment . . .'

Riley grinned. 'Hey, what if we get to

the crater lake and it's already bubbling?'

'Then I'll be racing you back to the bottom!' said Robert.

'It looks so smooth I bet you could slide down,' said Riley.

'I wonder if you'd get all the way to the bottom without wearing out the seat of your pants?' Robert pondered aloud.

'Now that is a scientific experiment we could definitely test out!' Riley said excitedly.

'Yeah, we need to do that – for science!' said Robert gleefully.

'Although, if the volcano was actually erupting, there's the risk that we'd get caught by flaming lava . . .' continued Riley in his most serious scientist voice, 'and who's going to believe the word of two kid scientists whose pants are actually on fire?'

Robert was laughing so hard that he had to stop for a minute to catch his breath and have a drink.

Still giggling, Riley plonked down beside him on a rock. Shrugging off his backpack, Riley took a swig from his water bottle.

Robert suddenly stopped laughing, his face growing serious. 'Riley, is there anybody looking at us?' he whispered.

Riley looked around. 'I don't think so. Why?'

'I'm just feeling a bit light-headed,' said Robert. 'It's probably nothing.'

'No way!' gasped Riley, already fearing the worst. 'Mate, you're just a bit dizzy. You've been talking non-stop and, at this altitude, I bet it's gone to your head. You're fine . . . just have some more water.'

Robert, smiling excitedly, took the

claw out of his pocket. With a resigned look, Riley grabbed Robert's arm and the two boys faded quietly away.

CHAPTER THREE

'You knew this would happen, didn't you?' Riley grumbled.

'How could I know?' said Robert, throwing his hands up in surrender. 'Blame the claw. You know I've got no control over it!'

'So, were there actually dinosaurs

in New Zealand? Is that what all the *probablys* were about earlier?' asked Riley, still grumpy.

Robert shrugged. 'I'm not sure. I just think it's odd that so few fossils have ever been found here. Only three or four bones in the whole country! Let's have a look around and as soon as we see water we'll go back, okay?'

'All right,' agreed Riley, looking around to see if there was anything large with big teeth he should be running away from.

The scene that faced them was different to any they had come across during their trips back to the prehistoric era. Lush green grass surrounded them on all sides. Dotted here and there were towering ferns and small stands of trees, some with flowers and blossoms spilling down. It looked just like a country meadow, edged on one side by a dark, dense pocket of rainforest.

'Wow, this is like paradise,' said Riley, impressed and relieved by the calm stillness around them.

'Look,' whispered Robert. 'Dinosaurs! Hundreds of them!'

All over the meadow were whole herds of enormous herbivores munching and grazing contentedly.

'Let's take a closer look,' said Robert, pulling out his voice recorder. 'I think that cute little guy just there is *Rhabdodon* (rab-doe-don). There's a herd of them grazing together and they look so peaceful, like a field of cows. Hey, Riley, this little one is coming over!'

Alarmed, Riley turned to see the approaching dinosaur.

Unlike Riley, Robert felt right at home. 'He's about the same height as Riley and me, so he must be quite a young one,' Robert continued speaking into his voice recorder. 'They walk on their hind legs, and this one has a really gentle face. Stay still, Riley, I think he's just curious.'

Riley stood frozen and wide-eyed as the *rhabdodon* stared hard at his face before giving him a good sniff. Riley leaned back, snapping a twig underfoot, which sent the young dinosaur skipping away to rejoin its herd.

'Wow! Don't tell me there are actually gentle, non-scary dinosaurs!' Riley said with a smile. 'It looked really smooth, just like the blue-tongue lizards at the zoo. So what else is there? Do you recognise

the others?' He was suddenly excited in spite of himself.

Robert swept his eyes across the meadow and pointed to a dinosaur at the edge of the forest. 'That little ankylosaur looks like *Struthiosaurus* (strew-thee-oh-sore-us). See how little it is? It's the smallest of the ankylosaurs, and it doesn't have the club tail like some of the bigger ones do. And that really huge 'saur next to it is a titanosaur of some kind – *Hypselosaurus* (hip-sel-lo-sore-us), I think. The first dinosaur eggs ever found were laid by one of them.' Robert paused and turned to Riley. 'But if that's what it is, then we're not in New Zealand at all!'

'If we're not in New Zealand, where are we?' said Riley. 'Or more importantly, *when* are we?'

'When should be easy,' Robert replied confidently. 'See all this grass? That only appeared during the middle of the Cretaceous period. Same with the flowers. But the huge size of the herds makes me think that it must be quite late in the Cretaceous, when overpopulation was a problem.'

Robert was in a world of his own and

would have been quite happy talking to himself for the rest of the day.

'So in your expert opinion, Professor Irwin . . . ?' asked Riley, trying to get to the point.

'Late Cretaceous Europe!' said Robert decisively. 'I can't believe all the species that are here! There are almost too many to count, and it's all so . . . calm. I wonder where all the predators are.'

Riley snorted. 'Let's just be glad they're not here!'

'Well, since we're always in such a rush to get out of here, let's make the most of our peaceful surroundings,' said Robert, marching off towards the dark, forested area with his voice recorder in hand.

With a roll of his eyes, Riley followed on behind him.

CHAPTER FOUR

Trailing behind Robert, Riley tried to look in every direction at once. Someone had to make sure they weren't being stalked by some awful meat-eating creature!

Robert was getting further and further ahead. Riley could barely hear Robert's excitable voice, getting quieter and quieter as Robert spoke into his voice recorder. 'Crikey, is that *Telmatosaurus* (tell-ma-toe-sore-us)? That looks like a nest! Look at the size of those eggs – they're bigger than rugby balls! They must have been laid by a *hypselosaurus . . .*'

Riley brushed aside a coppice of ferns and stepped through to find an idyllic little watering hole in front of him.

There was no sign of Robert. Riley hesitated, unsure of whether to keep going or to stay put. Since they needed water to return home, thought Riley, it wasn't a bad idea to stick close by. And though it was calm now, if a quick getaway was needed, Riley wanted to be ready for it.

Perching himself on a flat rock, Riley sat back and marvelled at the view. It was amazing – there was no doubt about it. Sure that Robert would soon return, Riley was almost relaxed as he watched the giant dragonflies flitting over the water.

Meanwhile, Robert marched on, recognising a different species of

dinosaur with almost every step. He spoke as fast as he could into his voice recorder, trying to note everything he would look up later. It occurred to Robert that he should have brought a video camera along. Next time, he thought, although he'd have a job on his hands trying to come up with a good reason for carrying a camera with him 24/7!

As he broke through the tree line, entering the darker patch of forest, Robert felt the temperature drop and goosebumps rising on his arms. Once he was through the thick barrier of trees, a huge clearing stretched out before him. The whole area was completely desolate, with blackened stumps where trees had once been.

'I wonder what's happened here,' Robert whispered to himself.

Any trees that were still there were barely standing, and no leaves or even a hint of green could be seen anywhere.

But it was the smell that was the worst! Robert could hardly breathe with the musty stench of mould and rot. He'd seen the aftermath of bushfires before, back home in Queensland, and knew the devastation they could cause. He wondered if that was what had happened here.

Robert was still taking in the grim scene when a sudden noise startled him. He threw himself on the ground, hoping that he hadn't been seen.

Robert inched forward on his stomach as well as he could. The ground was rocky and uneven, and there were huge dips and gashes that looked like they had been dug out by some gigantic creature.

Crawling over to the rim of the deepest pit, Robert could see a pack of about 20 small dinosaurs. Each was around the size of a chicken, and they were scurrying around on their two hind legs.

'Wow, *pyroraptors*!' Robert whispered to himself, dropping his voice recorder in excitement.

Twenty sharp, bird-eyed faces looked in his direction.

Robert froze, his heart racing. These guys were definitely carnivores. If he had to, Robert thought, he could fight off one or two of them. But 20?

To Robert's relief, the tiny dinosaurs turned back to what they were doing. The *pyroraptors* were clearly already very busy and, by the look of things, very well fed.

CHAPTER FIVE

Robert could hardly believe what he was seeing. The whole pit was teeming with the tiny carnivores picking their way through dozens of dinosaur carcasses. Some were fresh, newly killed dinosaurs and others had already been reduced to only their skeletons. No wonder there

had been no carnivores in the meadow –
there was plenty of food right here!

Robert had read about the elephant
graveyards in Africa, where elephants
instinctively went to die.

He wondered for a moment whether
dinosaurs did the same. But this scene
seemed different, and he couldn't shake
the feeling that some natural disaster
had occurred here, maybe more than
once. What else could have caused such
destruction?

A low rumbling noise suddenly
came from far away. Robert looked up,

expecting to see rain clouds overhead. But it wasn't thunder. By the time he looked back, the *pyroraptors* were fleeing in a single flock.

The calm of the meadow was shattered, and Robert could hear what sounded like a stampede heading his way. The gentle herbivores, so calm just minutes ago, were now swarming together and running full pelt for the cover of the forest.

'You're kidding! Is it an earthquake?' Robert uttered in disbelief.

There was another low rumble, this

time accompanied by a tremor so violent that Robert was knocked to the ground. Trees crashed all around, and everywhere he looked there were terrified dinosaurs, big and small, running in every direction. The noise was deafening.

Within a few moments the stampede had started to thin, with the slow, heavy sauropods bringing up the rear.

It was time to make a move. Robert took a deep breath and pulled himself to his feet. He had to get back to Riley. But before he could take so much as a single step, Robert found himself in the path of a panicked young *rhabdodon* that had been separated from its herd.

The deer-sized dinosaur didn't even pause. Robert felt the full weight of the *rhabdodon* as it ploughed into him, knocking him into the bone-filled pit.

CHAPTER SIX

Back at the waterhole, Riley was in a complete panic. He was all on his own with a bunch of rampaging dinosaurs, in the middle of an earthquake!

The dinosaurs were careering around all over the place, and he'd already seen a few major collisions that looked

45

pretty painful and possibly deadly.

Riley's main fear was that most of the dinosaurs appeared to be running towards the very place he'd last seen his best friend.

When the fourth tremor rippled across the meadow, stronger and longer than the one before it, Riley thought that he'd better get moving. Something must have happened, otherwise Robert would surely be running straight for him and the water right about now.

Or now ... Riley thought, counting to ten.

Or now . . .

Nope, it wasn't happening.

There was no point waiting any longer. Robert must be in trouble, and Riley was going to have to find out where. He crossed his fingers for luck and, looking wistfully back at his lovely watering hole, headed for the forest.

The tremors came every few minutes, and Riley was convinced they were building up to something even bigger.

'Robert! Rob-ert!' Riley yelled as he ran. Ducking and diving and sprinting and swerving, Riley made his way into the forest without injury. There were a lot of dinosaurs down, and some were limping along, injured.

Between tremors there was a kind of eerie silence, as though the earth itself was bracing for the next one. During one such lull, after looking under rocks and fallen trees for what seemed like ages, Riley thought he heard something.

'Ri-ley! Riley, is that you?' Robert yelled at the top of his lungs.

Riley ran towards the sound of Robert's voice. 'Mate, am I glad to see you. I thought you were a goner!'

'I'm over here!' called Robert. 'I can't get out!'

'How did you end up down there?' said Riley, peering over the edge of the pit.

'I'll tell you the whole story later, but first, I need help getting out of here before anything else lands on me. My ankle's twisted and I can't stand on it. Any ideas?' Robert asked hopefully.

'No problem. Don't forget that I am a boy scout,' said Riley, though right now he felt anything but prepared.

Riley climbed down carefully into the pit, relieved to find Robert in one piece. Putting his first-aid badge to good use, he quickly figured out that Robert's swollen ankle was badly bruised but not broken. Scavenging around in the pit wasn't for the faint-hearted, but Riley came back with two long bones and a length of vine.

In a few minutes, Robert's leg was supported by a tidy-looking splint. With Robert leaning on Riley for support, the boys slowly made their way out of the pit.

'Should we head back to the water?' asked Riley, gasping for breath. 'Or did you want to drop in on anyone else?'

Robert grinned and elbowed him in the ribs.

Riley laughed, then grew serious. 'I can't believe this is happening,' he said, shaking his head.

'When you think about it, it makes sense,' said Robert, as they slowly hobbled back towards the watering hole. 'I mean, this is really late in the Cretaceous period. And scientists reckon that there would have been more and more natural disasters before the extinction of the dinosaurs, caused by major changes in the climate. There would have been earthquakes and huge forest fires, volcanic eruptions and tsunamis for thousands of years before the asteroid hit! Don't forget that the next ice age was just around the corner.'

'That's not what I was talking about,' answered Riley, laughing. 'I meant that I can't believe we are in the middle of an earthquake and that you nearly broke your ankle!'

'Oh.' Robert looked sheepish. He had a tendency to get carried away when it came to dinosaurs.

As another tremor shook the earth, the boys hobbled faster. The angry rumblings were coming thick and fast now, and both boys were worried that a full-blown earthquake wasn't far away.

As they reached the waterhole, it was hard not to see the changes that had taken place in the space of only a few minutes.

The idyllic meadow was now empty of wildlife, and the trees and plants that were still standing looked dark and menacing. Holding hands, Robert and

Riley threw themselves into the water, and relief and dizziness whisked them away.

CHAPTER SEVEN

'Okay, so that has to be our luckiest escape ever!' declared Robert, as he and Riley struggled to catch their breath.

'Crikey,' said Riley, before they both collapsed into a heap of hysterical giggles.

'You could have been seriously

injured,' said Riley, once their laughing fit had passed.

'I know,' said Robert. 'I really thought my ankle was broken there for a while. But, look, it's so much better already! And it only took 65 million years or so!' he said, taking off the splint. 'Lucky you knew how to strap it up. I didn't realise you were such a fantastic boy scout!'

'Shame there isn't a badge for earthquake survival,' joked Riley.

'Or prehistoric first aid,' said Robert.

'Or time travel,' added Riley.

'Or dinosaur hunting.'

56

Riley grinned. 'Or running away from dinosaurs.'

'Hey, I thought these were just sticks!' said Robert, looking down at the splint in his hands. 'They're bones! Leg bones, by the look of them. Look at how long they are! And they must be nearly 70 million years old – unbelievable!' he said. 'I can't believe we've brought them all the way from the Cretaceous period. I wonder which dinosaur they're from.'

Robert was beside himself with excitement. They'd never brought any-thing back with them before. Robert

57

started seeing visions of the museums he could fill and the skeletons he could rebuild. He'd be a world-famous palaeontologist before he was even grown up!

Riley sat there silently, looking around. 'Umm . . . Robert? I don't think we're home.'

'What?' said Robert, glancing up at Riley. 'Of course we are, where else would we be? There's Mount Doom right over there, quietly smoking away.'

'Do you remember *our* Mount Doom quietly smoking away?' asked Riley. 'Do you think your mum would have let us climb an active volcano that was actually *smoking*? And where's the chairlift? Where's the rest of the group? And what are *they*?'

Riley was now on his feet, pointing down the mountain, and his voice was getting more and more shrill.

Below them on the lush green lowlands was a scene similar to the one they'd just left. Dinosaurs of all shapes and sizes were fleeing the mountain.

'Wow!' said Robert. 'Hadrosaurs, ceratopsians, titanosaurs and, look, that could even be an allosaur! This is New Zealand though, right? I mean, isn't that Mount Ruapehu?'

Riley squinted into the distance. 'I think so. Maybe we've come back to the right place but in the wrong time?'

'That's exactly what I was thinking,' agreed Robert. 'The ground is still covered in the lush green of the Cretaceous. And I can't see any snow, even at the top of the mountains.'

'So there *were* dinosaurs in New Zealand?' asked Riley, confused.

'Not just a few, either,' said Robert.

'It looks like there were just as many here as there were everywhere else we've been. But where are they all going?'

'Away from here,' Riley said grimly.

The boys turned around just in time to see a group of feathered, chicken-sized raptors running down the hill towards them at speed.

'*Compsognathuses* (comp-sog-nay-thuss-ez)?' yelled Robert in disbelief.

Riley's face turned white as a sheet. 'Are they going to attack us?'

But the *compsognathuses* didn't so much as slow down as they raced past,

leaving the boys in no doubt that the dinosaurs were utterly terrified. What were they so afraid of?

Robert and Riley nervously looked to the mountain top just a kilometre or two away, and watched the pale grey trickle of smoke turn into a billowing black cloud. They could almost feel the pressure building beneath their feet and, without a word or a look between them, Robert and Riley turned and ran.

CHAPTER EIGHT

Glancing back, Robert could see the red-hot lava spewing from the volcano as it began to erupt.

'Whatever you do, Riley, don't look back!' Robert yelled.

Riley glanced behind them and immediately wished he hadn't. The volcano was now shooting molten rock and magma hundreds of metres in the air, while rivers of lava were snaking their way down, igniting everything in their path.

Riley let out a yelp and ran faster. 'You're right, I didn't want to see that!'

With magma missiles landing all around them, the boys zigzagged their way past freshly made ditches and crashed through woodland, emptied of all signs of life.

The *compsognathuses* were nowhere to be seen. It was clear that any creatures that were once here had already fled the area.

'How are we going to get home?' spluttered Riley.

Robert coughed, his mouth dry from breathing in the volcanic ash. 'I'm not sure,' he replied, breathing hard. 'There doesn't seem to be any water around here, but don't worry, we always find a way!'

Just as he said this, the boys hit a dip in the track and, in perfect unison, fell headlong into a ditch of wet, sticky mud.

When they opened their eyes, Robert and Riley found themselves lying under a sprinkling of freshly fallen snow. They glanced up at the top of Mount Ruapehu. Covered by a thin layer of snow, the tip of the mountain was smoke-free. Robert and Riley sighed with relief.

'Crikey,' said Robert, 'that was close.'

'At least the volcano isn't erupting this time,' said Riley. 'But where are we now? Just tell me it's not the ice age!'

Within seconds, Terri and Bindi came

round the corner. They were accompanied by a couple of other walkers and the second guide, who was speaking into her walkie-talkie and looking a bit concerned.

'Ah, Robert, Riley!' said Terri. 'I told you, Bindi, they're such sensible boys. I knew you'd stop once the snow started. It's a freak weather change but apparently snow's quite common here all the year round!'

'The guides are going to round up the whole group and take us back down,' explained Bindi. 'They reckon it wouldn't be safe to carry on up without the proper climbing gear.'

'It's such a shame, and we have to go home tomorrow,' said Terri. 'Looks like we'll have to come back another time to see the crater lake, boys. I hope you're not too disappointed.'

Robert and Riley glanced nervously at the summit again, half expecting to see smoke rising out of it.

'No, no, that's fine!' Robert said cheerfully. 'So there's no problem with the volcano itself?'

'It's not going to erupt or anything?' added Riley.

Terri and Bindi looked at each other with raised eyebrows and smiled.

'I think we might just make it down before she blows,' said Terri, 'if we're quick!'

The boys didn't need telling twice. And even though they knew that Terri was joking, they thought speed wouldn't be a bad idea at all.

CHAPTER NINE

As they drove south, Terri had never seen the boys so quiet. She knew how disappointed they must be feeling, having come all this way and having been so excited about seeing the crater lake, only to have their plans dashed at the last moment. If only there was some way to make it up to them, she thought.

'Are we there already?' Robert said sleepily, when they pulled into a car park.

'I thought we'd take a little detour,' said Terri, with a wink at Bindi. 'This is Hawke's Bay on the east coast of the North Island. The guidebook says there's an interesting museum here, so it should be a good spot for us to stretch our legs.'

'Hawke's Bay?' said Robert. 'Why does that sound familiar?'

'Oh, I don't know,' Terri said with a grin. 'Maybe because it's one of the only places in New Zealand where dinosaur fossils have ever been found?'

'Awesome!' Brightening immediately, Robert couldn't get out of the car fast enough.

Riley rolled his eyes and followed suit.

The Irwins and Riley entered the quiet museum. Though the fossil display wasn't a big one, the curator was friendly and was clearly pleased to have visitors.

'You know, until today I didn't realise that New Zealand even had dinosaurs,' said Riley, as they looked over the single cabinet of fossils that had been found in the area.

'Well, for a long time, everyone thought that,' replied the curator. 'Then Joan Wiffen, a local woman from just up the road, started finding them all over the Maungahouanga Valley.'

'Was she a palaeontologist?' asked Robert.

The curator shook his head. 'Not at all. She just seemed to know the right places to look.'

'So which dinosaurs are they from?' asked Riley.

'That's the mystery,' said the curator, with a glint in his eye. 'There's only one or two bones from any single dinosaur, so scientists don't really know exactly which species they belong to. We need to find a lot more bones before we'll be able to put them together and find the answer.'

'So Hawke's Bay would be a great place for someone starting out as a palaeontologist?' asked Robert.

'Maybe, maybe not,' said the curator. 'There are plenty of people, scientists included, who still claim that there were no dinosaurs in the whole of New Zealand and that these bones just made their way here by sea from who knows where.'

'But there were dinosaurs here! There were loads of them!' said Robert earnestly, earning quizzical looks from Bindi and Terri.

'Ha, how would you know, Robert?' said Riley, laughing nervously. 'You haven't seen them, have you?'

'Very funny, Riley,' said Robert as the others laughed.

'Well, between you and me, that's what I think, too!' said the curator. If he was surprised by Robert's outburst, he didn't show it.

Robert and Riley carried on around the museum, looking at local artefacts and reading all there was about Joan Wiffen. But they kept returning to the single cabinet of fossils.

'I just can't believe there are so few of them when so many palaeontologists have spent their whole lives looking,' said Robert. 'Imagine how many times we could fill this whole museum if we had brought back all the bones we saw today!'

Robert looked thoughtful. He took the fossilised claw from his back pocket and studied it. 'We could be the most famous and successful palaeontologists ever!'

'We?' said Riley, not looking convinced.

'Not even just palaeontologists, Riley!' Robert was on a roll. 'We could bring back real live dinosaurs, like on that TV show. We could be the only real-life dinosaur hunters in the world!

And we could have our own dinosaur zoo!'

'Now *that* I like the sound of,' said Riley, deciding that being a dinosaur zookeeper with his best friend would probably be the best job ever.

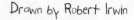

Drawn by Robert Irwin

PYRORAPTOR

GENUS: *Pyroraptor olympius*

ETYMOLOGY: *Pyroraptor olympius* means 'Olympic fire thief'. 'Pyro' is Greek for 'fire' and 'raptor' is Latin for 'thief'

DISCOVERED: Just a handful of bones from a single specimen were found by Ronan Allain and Philippe Taquet in 1992 in Provence, southern France

PERIOD: Late Cretaceous period, approximately 70 million years ago

LENGTH: 1.6 metres long

HEIGHT: 60 centimetres tall

WEIGHT: Up to about 30 kilograms

DIET: Even though *pyroraptor* was a small dinosaur, it was a carnivore and would have eaten insects, lizards and small mammals

Pyroraptor was a little theropod dinosaur about the size of a chicken, and it's quite probable that it was feathered like one, too. It was quick and agile, running on two legs, with a long tail that would have helped it to balance. Like many of the raptors, it had strong limbs and a large curved claw on the second toe of each foot that may have been used as a weapon or to help with climbing, like a grappling hook. This claw was 6.5 centimetres long, so *pyroraptor* wasn't one to mess with!

Pyroraptor didn't earn its name from an ability to breathe fire, steal fire or even walk across hot coals. Allain and Taquet chose the name because *pyroraptor's* fossilised remains were discovered in the aftermath of a forest fire.

HOW DID DINOSAURS BECOME EXTINCT?

Scientists know that dinosaurs became extinct at the end of the Cretaceous period, around 65 million years ago. But what caused this? The most popular theories about the extinction of dinosaurs can be divided into two main groups.

Some scientists believe that one catastrophic event — a meteorite crashing into Earth — was responsible for the extinction of dinosaurs.

A few crater sites have been put forward as possible impact zones. The Chictulub Crater in the Yucatán Peninsula, Mexico is the most likely site, measuring

200 kilometres wide. The Shiva Crater at the India-Seychelles rift is another alternative. When it was first formed, the Shiva Crater would have been 600 kilometres long and 450 kilometres wide!

On the opposite end of the scale are 'gradualists', who believe that the extinction of dinosaurs was caused by climate change and high volcanic activity over millions of years.

The Deccan Traps in India is one example of the large-scale eruptions that were frequent towards the end of the Cretaceous period.

Spanning 800,000 square kilometres, its beds of volcanic basalt were formed when huge volumes of lava were released from a series of eruptions that occurred over thousands of years.

Experts do agree that the end of the Cretaceous period was characterised by major changes in the biosphere, which led to global firestorms, earthquakes, tsunamis, acid rain and the collapse of food chains.

But there will probably never be a definitive answer about what caused the extinction of dinosaurs due to the lack of fossils and sample sites from the end of the Cretaceous period.

COLLECT THE SERIES

Interested in finding out what
Robert does when he's not
hunting dinosaurs?

Check out www.australiazoo.com.au

Loved the book?

There's so much more
stuff to check out online